I'm Single, Not Sorry

Jennifer L. Payne

ISBN: 979-8-218-02675-2

Author: Jennifer L. Payne
Editor: Marni MacRae
Illustrator: Juan Roberts/Creative Lunacy

Dedication

This book is dedicated to my best friend, the person who told me I was past my prime, halfway over the hill. Thank you for the motivation. You know who you are. Love you, always.

Acknowledgement

I thank my **mom and dad** for never giving up on me and making me into the woman I am today. I hated it when I was young, but I especially thank my mom for the home-schooled English lessons, typing classes, and writing assignments she made me do in addition to regular schoolwork. I'm finally seeing the fruit from that labor. I love you both beyond measure!

I thank my only child, **my son**, for loving me unconditionally and allowing me to be his mom even when I wasn't at my best. I'm still learning and growing. I love you beyond comprehension. You are my world!

Thank you **DaNietra Hall** for being on this crazy journey with me from the beginning. My Inspector Gadget, it's been a helluva ride, but you stayed on to the end. Love ya!

Shana McClain, you've known me since I was 14 – every relationship, every hookup, every wild ride … you know what it is. Love ya!

Tasha White, even with the time difference, you answered. Thank you for the late-night ear, being my soundboard, shoulder, and cheerleader!

To the **men** I've dated, been in a relationship with, those who have done me wrong and broke my heart, thank you for the inspiration!

To my **Detroit** friends turned family, thank you for all your love and support. I love y'all!

Table of Contents

Introducing Ava Amore & Friends

Being a woman feels a lot like being a carton of eggs in the grocery store. When you're new and fresh, nearly everyone wants to pick you up and take you home. However, when you're nearing your "expiration date," the one a stranger stamped on you the moment you arrived at the market, you begin to get left behind. After all, no one wants to buy old, rotten eggs, deemed worthless after the window of freshness has elapsed. Instead, they end up in the trash. There's nothing wrong with that, of course, when we're actually talking about eggs. The problem arises when the same attitude is applied to a human being.

Society tells women that we have essentially passed our expiration date when we become a certain age. *ScienceDaily* reported that, when asked how they felt about being older and single, unmarried women of a certain age felt both "highly visible and invisible. Heightened visibility came from feelings of exposure and invisibility came from assumptions made by others."

As we age, there is the idea that women become less attractive, whether it be from smile lines that mark the passage of time or the natural decline in our ability to bear life. Like groceries, single women lose their "freshness" once they reach their mid to late thirties—our supposed prime.

We lose the young, naive glimmer in our eyes that once signaled to men across the bar that we could be easily wooed with a drink and an empty promise. We lose the slim frame of a still-developing body, trading it for the womanly shape of a Botticelli muse. Along with these losses, we also lose the interest of prospective partners. Someone younger and prettier can effortlessly come along to take our place. How are we supposed to compete in an ever-losing battle against time and aging?

A woman's "prime" is supposed to be our best opportunity to get our lives in order and follow that path that's been laid out before us. Find a partner, fall in love, get married, start a family, become a mom. This is the standard formula for a supposed perfect life, the ritual all girls must go through once they reach adulthood. As if there is no other way to live life correctly. Not to mention, we've only got fifteen years to figure out who we want to spend the rest of our lives with and what that life looks like. Even if fifteen years sounds like a sufficient amount of time, don't forget that ten of those years are spent in our twenties, when no one even knows who they are. If we don't know who we are, how is anyone expected to figure out the rest of their lives in that small amount of time? So, in reality, it's only about five years to figure out what we're looking for in a partner, find that person, and fall in love, lest we reach our expiration date alone and risk losing that opportunity forever. Easy, right?

As we age, we're often consumed by this pressure in life. According to that same *ScienceDaily* article, many unmarried women confess that they feel as if their time is "running out." We're running out of time to fall in love, get married, and get pregnant. As more couples marry and others begin their ruthless commentary on our timelines, it's no wonder why so many women constantly feel the crushing weight of expectation.

So, what happens if someone decides not to conform to this social pressure? What if we use our "prime" differently? What if someone rejects the notion that their time is up and decides to write their own story instead of playing the tragic heroine society so desperately wants her to be?

Well, that's precisely what I, Ava Amore, decided to do.

When it came to these societal norms about how I was supposed to live my life, I firmly said no. I wasn't going to live my life any other way than exactly how I wanted. No one was going to force me into a stupid box. I was going to do whatever I wanted, screw whoever I wanted, fall in love, and have my heart broken as many times as I wanted, for as long as I wanted to. And that was how I happily lived my life through my twenties and thirties. Not even for a single day did I live for anyone other than me.

Despite the leper-like stigma surrounding being single and older, I have found so much joy in my life by choosing myself first. Whatever I wanted, I went after it, and more often than not, I got it. It wasn't that I didn't care about love or never planned on getting married, but rather I wanted to focus on my personal growth as a new adult and build a lasting and successful career for myself first instead.

However, that didn't mean that the journey was easy. As a woman who didn't follow these social norms, you have no idea how many times I had to stop and ask myself, "Ava Amore, are you sure this is worth it?"

There were indeed times I wondered if I was crazy for putting my career first over finding love. But, no matter how many times I questioned myself, my heart always brought me back to the same conclusion.

"Yes, it is worth it. I am worth it."

On nights when I was a little less sure, in my early twenties, I used to turn to the internet to see what people online had to say. Yes, there is an endless sea of articles and videos telling you that life sucks when you're older and unmarried, but there is also a surprising amount of support and justification for choosing a different lifestyle. This is where I found comfort that cemented the foundation to the certainty of my decisions. 30seconds.com listed feelings of liberation, knowing better what you want, and enjoyment in living alone as reasons we as women shouldn't worry about finding love later in life. Articles and blog posts like these made me feel empowered as I read them, proving that I didn't have to live my life a certain way just because other people thought I needed to. Everyone was different, so why weren't we all allowed to make different decisions?

I firmly held onto my beliefs for twenty long years and ignored anyone who told me I needed to "go on just one more blind date" or "sign up for a dating app before it was too late for me." Never once did my mind waiver, because I knew my well-being was worth more than anything any man could give me.

Of course, there were still times when words from my family and friends cut me deeply. I was powerful but not bulletproof. When you step outside the box, you also lose the walls that once protected you. How was I expected never to be affected when I had a million people in my ear telling me I was losing my value as a woman the longer I chose to stay unmarried? When I was constantly reminded that my expiration date was soon arriving and no one would buy a spoiled carton of eggs? As if my worth was only as much as attaching myself to another person and becoming a vessel for a new life.

There were days when these hurtful words pierced through my steel armor and broke me down. These days made it especially hard to watch couples who looked into their partner's eyes and saw a "forever" when I could only look ahead into uncertainty. Unfortunately, my fortieth birthday was one of those nights.

"Happy birthday to you, happy birthday to you! Happy birthday dear Ava, happy birthday to you!" My four best friends sang to me, swaying back and forth with raised drinks, their pitchy performance drawing attention from the other patrons of the swanky sushi bar. Nearby tables joined in with joyful clapping, making my cheeks flush with embarrassment, but I was appreciative for the positive energy. When it came to turning forty, I needed all the help I could get to shake off the strange feeling that had been brewing within for weeks leading up to the big day. I wasn't sad or feeling down, per se, yet there was almost an invisible wall between me and my happiness now that I was another year older. It was the first time I'd ever felt this way, and the feelings knocked at the back of my mind during my birthday celebration.

"Make a wish!" Leeta squealed excitedly as she leaned in and propped her chin against both hands, her dark eyes gleaming with hope.

"She's too old for that, come on," Hannah scowled, waving one hand dismissively while the other brought her glass of chardonnay to her lips.

"You're never too old to make a wish." Leeta beamed, completely ignoring Hannah's negativity, as usual. Even at the age of forty, Leeta was the most positive, optimistic, and hopeful person I'd ever met in my life. No obstacle or setback was significant or traumatic enough to bring her unwavering positivity down. It was one of the many reasons I was grateful to have her as a friend.

I blew out the candles before Hannah or the other ladies could make another comment. It was just a simple birthday candle—nothing over the top, nothing special.

I'd never put too much pressure or weight on my birthdays until that day. All I wanted was to spend my birthday with my best friends, since we no longer got the chance to see each other as often as we used to when we were younger. Of course, we didn't spend every birthday together, but this year was different for me. It was as if a magical, optimistic switch in my brain turned off and a PA system turned on, blaring out the same message over and over.

"You're old."

Whether they knew it or not, just having them around was the best support I could have asked for on my birthday.

"What did you wish for?" Leeta whispered as she leaned closer to me. Her long, light brown hair nearly landed in her empty plate of food.

"Oh my goodness, Leeta. Are you still on that?" Sidney groaned and rolled her eyes. Her dry and sarcastic nature was the polar opposite of Leeta's cheerfulness. "You make me need another drink," she added as she drained the last of her strawberry mojito.

"Amen to that!" Hannah replied, raising her drink and clinking glasses with Sidney's empty mojito.

"I wished for you all to stop fighting," I shot back playfully as I looked around the table at my four best friends.

On the right side of the table was sarcastic Sidney, an extremely tall, caramel-complexioned, forty-two-year-old with dyed honey-blonde hair. Beside her was Nina, who was a forty-three-year-old woman with jet black hair, styled in a bob so sharp it could cut diamonds, wearing a freshly pressed blazer suit. Nina wasn't the type of woman to tolerate anything not "up to her standard," which was a high bar to reach, so I could always count on her to look impeccable.

On my left was Leeta, who was basically the forty-year-old woman version of a Care Bear with long brown hair, dimples, and a fondness for wearing long skirts and sandals in all types of weather. Last but not least, beside Leeta sat Hannah, the youngest of the five of us. Her naturally blonde hair and blue eyes, in combination with her baby face and petite frame, made her look innocent to anyone who didn't know her, but her resting "B" face and sharp tongue made her anything but sweet.

I met Sidney, Nina, and Leeta in college while working as servers at the local dinner down the street from our university. We quickly grew close, bonding over our side work and post-shift drinks at the bar around the corner. To say that I'd known them for over twenty years still blew my mind.

Hannah, on the other hand, I'd known since middle school and have always had quite a complex relationship with her, due to her often hateful nature. Despite her inner mean girl, though, Hannah was still someone so close to me that I considered her my sister. During our sophomore year of college, when Hannah started looking for a part-time job, I recommended her to the diner I worked at, and thus the era of our friendship as five blossomed. Together, the five of us had trekked through the highs and lows of our twenties, thirties, and now forties.

Between us were decades worth of history, memories, and sisterhood.

"Is there anything else you wanted to do to celebrate your birthday, Ava?" Hannah asked as she cleared her throat and stared at me. Her bright blue eyes reminded me of a cloudless sky in the middle of spring. Looking into them always calmed me down. I was pretty sure that natural calming effect was how I was able to survive the last thirty years with Hannah and her sandpaper personality.

"She just took one bite of her cake! Ask her later," Nina hissed across the table and eyed Hannah like a stern mother scolding her child. The irony of their behavior made me chuckle, since Hannah herself was a mother to one child, whereas Nina had none.

"It's already nine o'clock, and Sara needs me to tuck her into bed every night or else she can't sleep," Hannah explained to the table, subtly directing her attention primarily to Nina.

"It's just one night," Nina reasoned. It looked like Hannah was preparing to snap back when I interrupted the conversation, doing my best to negate another little fight.

"Don't worry. There's nothing else planned," I said, my smile feeling forced. "We can get the check now and head back. Hannah's right, it is getting late. Sidney and Hannah have kids and we all have work tomorrow, but I really appreciate you guys all coming out, especially on a Thursday. I love you, girls!"

I raised my glass of Pinot Grigio in an attempt to uplift the mood. Dinner had gone so well until the end, but I suppose nine o'clock was the witching hour when you have kids or a husband to get back home to.

"We love you too, Ava," the girls cheered as we clinked glasses together one last time. We all finished the last of our drinks before I flagged down a server for our check and to-go boxes. After packing up our dinner and signing the receipt, we exited the packed restaurant in a single file line, weaving our way between countless tables and bar seats.

As we squeezed out the front door, we passed a large group of twenty-something-year-olds, huddled by the hostess stand in a cluster, waiting for their table with flushed cheeks and infectiously rambunctious energy.

I chuckled to myself as I turned the corner, as it reminded me of my days when I was younger, having dinner at nine to soak up the alcohol from the pregame before going for round two.

Watching the girls gave me a momentary rush of indefinable emotion because up until today, I had almost felt like I was still one of them. Even throughout my thirties, I'd had that "invincible youth" blood coursing through my veins; but now that I was officially forty, it was as if my hot blood had gone cold. Now, I was left only with a metallic aftertaste on my tongue.

I brushed off the feeling and followed my friends outside, putting on a brave smile to convince myself more than anyone else that turning forty was fine. No one else seemed phased by the young women, after all.

We stopped in the middle of a parking aisle and started to pair off to hug each other goodbye. I never expected when growing older how infrequently I would see my friends compared to my twenties and thirties. It was no longer as simple as walking over to someone's dorm or meeting every weekend to go bar hopping anymore. Truthfully, it was primarily spamming texts in the group chat to stay involved in each other's lives or trying to arrange a plan with five vastly different schedules for a get-together once every few months, at best. It was a bittersweet feeling having to say goodbye. I was so happy to see all of my best friends on the birthday I needed them the most, but I wasn't ready for them to disappear yet. Still, I understood that everyone had somewhere to go or someone to be with, instead of having the freedom to be spontaneous, so I held my tongue and bit my lip.

I gave each of my friends a big hug, clumsily maneuvering around the armload of gifts. Each bag was suspiciously tall, slim, and heavy, so I could already imagine what each of them got me. Then, we walked our separate ways toward our cars and gave each other a final wave before peeling out of the parking lot and driving away. I watched them drive off as I sat in my car, keys dangling from the ignition, feeling a sense of emptiness slowly creep into my chest.

"Forty..." I mumbled to myself. I couldn't wrap my head around the idea. For thirty-nine years, birthdays had come and gone so naturally, without a second thought, but now it was as if all those years had suddenly piled up all at once, the pressure of them weighing on me in an unfamiliar way. There was a part of me that never really thought turning forty was real. I knew that sounded crazy, but when I used to think of the number forty, it always felt so far away. It sounded so middle-aged. Anyone in their twenties was undeniably young, people in their thirties were considered mature, but people in their forties were just plain old.

I turned on my car and slowly pulled out of my parking spot to head home. While gripping the steering wheel, I exhaled a heavy sigh and drove away from the restaurant onto the freeway.

Finally, after twenty minutes of stewing in my own negativity, I arrived at the designated parking spot for my townhouse and pulled in. Although I was very much capable of buying a home, it never made sense to buy a big house just to live in all by myself. My cozy townhouse felt much more suitable. I made my way up the stairs, unlocked the door, and turned on the light. It was quiet and chilly inside, and the empty space seemed more cavernous than when I had left it.

The living room was minimalist with a three-seat couch, matching oversized chair, coffee table, and a 70-inch TV mounted above an entertainment system. The walls were lined with large windows, framed by white shutters, and the ceilings were tall, with recessed lighting. To the left of the living room was the kitchen, which had dark, cool-toned brown cabinets with silver fixtures and white granite countertops.

I set the gift bags onto the kitchen counter and pulled away tufts of tissue paper to reveal four bottles of well-aged red wine, to the surprise of no one. Each bottle looked equally tasty, so I chose one at random, uncorked it, and grabbed a glass. I had a four-piece wine glass set, despite living alone, for the sake of having wine with guests. When I'd bought them, I hadn't expected to have company over so infrequently. I confidently poured myself a glass without even looking down. The movement was familiar, as enjoying wine on the couch was a frequent weekend ritual, so I had no fear of spilling. I crossed my legs and leaned back on my oversized chair, taking a sip of the rich, red liquid as I closed my eyes. Notes of cherry and black currant filled my nose and mouth and I let out a deep sigh.

I opened my eyes and glanced over at my three-seat couch. For an instant, I envisioned a man sitting there beside me, a soft smile on his handsome, rugged face. I blinked hard and looked away, shaking off the thought. Perhaps my drinking tolerance had suddenly declined with my turning forty, or the devilish whispers throughout the day were finally getting to me now that I was alone with my thoughts. There was nothing I would have wanted to trade my twenties and thirties for, I reminded myself. My priorities were my freedom and my achievements. I loved that I never had to "report" to someone else about where I was going or who I was going with. It was just that simple. When everyone else was chasing lovers who didn't treat them right, I found happiness and security within myself, and that's precisely how I got myself to where I was now. But if I was that happy and secure, why was I suddenly feeling so down about myself on my birthday?

Not once, before tonight, had I compared myself to my friends when it came to how all of our lives turned out. Yet somehow, here I was, sitting in my living room, second-guessing the decisions of my younger self, wondering how it felt for them to come home to their partners and families that night. Moonlight filtered in between the gaps in the shutters, illuminating the living room with cool, dim light. It might have been romantic, in another context.

When we were in college, my friends and I were all in the same place together, yet we all diverged so dramatically twenty years later. There was Sidney, who was always the instigator when it came to relationships and gossip. No topic was off the table for her, no matter how personal it was. Funnily enough, her excessively sarcastic nature made it easier to talk about vulnerable issues since she had a way of making things seem less serious than they really were. She was the first of us to get married, just a few years after graduating college. When Sidney announced that she was engaged, her voice had been so monotone and her composure so calm and collected that we had all dismissed it as a joke. It wasn't until we saw the ring on her hand that we believed it to be real. I hated to even think it, but I'd always suspected something wasn't quite right between Sidney and her husband. It was as if Sidney had settled for the first guy who wanted to tie her down; but then again, who am I to judge when they have seventeen years of marriage and two kids under their belt?

It was another ten years before anyone else got married. Nina, who we all secretly thought would get married first, had always been a bit of a know-it-all and an undeniable perfectionist. From her home to her husband to her upbringing, there wasn't a single thing that wasn't "perfect." However, none of this masked the troubles we all knew had been boiling underneath the surface of her flawless facade. In all our years of friendship, though, no one had been able to gather enough courage to confront her about it.

Hannah and Leeta, on the other hand, were closer to my own situation. Although Hannah already had a child, her ex-boyfriend was no longer in the picture. He left halfway through the pregnancy, so she raised her daughter Sara all by herself. Leeta was neither married nor had children, like me. Despite her troubling dating history with men who tended to take advantage of her kindness, instead of treasuring her pure heart, Leeta had never let her dating failures shake her confidence or destroy her dream of one day getting married.

Even though two of my best friends were also unmarried, I still somehow felt alienated. As if my aloneness was lonelier than their own. I knew it wasn't healthy nor productive to compare my life to others, but there was clearly something in the wine that was making me act differently. Turning forty was supposed to be like any other birthday, yet here I was, running through a cycle of unproductive thoughts about my love life. I was shocked at how much my confidence was shaken, based on nothing more than two little numbers.

Just yesterday, I couldn't have cared less if someone stared at me as I enjoyed dinner alone or took myself on a date to the movies. I was happy living outside the confines of expectation. But once the clock struck midnight and my fortieth birthday had begun, my entire world came crashing down around me. When I woke up that morning, it was as if the wrinkles in my face were deeper, my ringless hand was naked, and my cozy little townhouse was unnervingly empty. I didn't even have a dog to come home to. All I had to keep me company was my wine and the moonlight.

"Am I really past my prime now that I'm forty?" I pondered aloud as I swirled my wine around the glass, watching it lap against the edges like the waves of a burgundy sea. Then, I exhaled slowly, blowing a strand of hair out of my eyes and sinking deeper into my seat. I couldn't believe the day I fell weak to society's pressure had finally come.

I tried to remind myself of my worth, running through a checklist of positive qualities and proud accomplishments, none of which I would have if I had wasted my time in a dead-end relationship with a subpar man. I'm a highly successful and well-respected executive at the company I work for, and I'm thriving in my entrepreneurial endeavors as well. I'm healthy, an amazing cook, work out, and have regular attendance at my local gym—but don't get it twisted, I still make a mean mac 'n cheese and 7-up pound cake, and enjoy eating them too! I even made sure to stay in check with my emotional well-being. On paper, I was easily someone's dream woman. Hell, I'm my own dream woman. Yet here I was, moping on my birthday about being single and alone.

I squeezed my eyes shut tightly and tried to summon younger Ava, who didn't care about what anyone thought about her and would have had a witty comeback to the self-deprecating voice that gnawed at my subconscious. She must have been busy, though, because I couldn't reach her. I downed the rest of my wine and poured myself another glass immediately. Normally, I don't drink this much or this fast, but today is different. I deserve to live a little on my birthday, I justified.

As my mood threatened to sour further, I tried to summon some fire from within. Like a mantra, I began to repeat my repertoire of inspiring quotes that I'd committed to memory throughout the years. Lada Gaga once said, "some women choose to follow men, and some women choose to follow their dreams. If you're wondering which way to go, remember that your career will never wake up and tell you that it doesn't love you anymore."

Throughout my career, this quote has been my biggest supporter. I committed it to memory and internalized the meaning as if etching it in stone. Back then, my classmates, coworkers, and even my best friends were all going the nine yards to find a boyfriend or girlfriend, except for me. For as hard as they were working to find love, I worked twice as hard to find an excellent job to jumpstart my career as a businesswoman and to also become an entrepreneur. Of course, I still wanted someone to love me and stand by my side through my ups and downs, just as much as the next person. It's human nature, after all. The difference was, finding that person wasn't as high on my list of priorities as it seemed to be for everyone else. I dated and flirted and put myself out there when I had the time, but it never worked out, or they were never worth what I had to give up in exchange. I probably even broke some hearts along the way.

I threw my head back again and swallowed the rest of my second glass of wine, feeling the warmth rush to my head.

"A busy, vibrant, goal-oriented woman is so much more attractive than a woman who waits around for a man to validate her existence," Mandy Hale advised. I said the words aloud, forcing myself to believe them.

As I moved through my twenties, I had become even less interested in following the conventional timeline I saw so many other women succumb to. Instead, my energy was focused solely on moving up the corporate ladder. Sure, as I jogged through the park my eyes would catch couples celebrating their anniversaries over a picnic or sharing a quiet cup of coffee cuddled on a bench, but I never wanted it enough to put myself and my dreams second. Never, until tonight. Now that I was feeling a little tipsy, my third glass of wine went down even more smoothly than the first two. Whoever got me this bottle of cabernet had great taste. Now I was feeling loose and let my hair down, running my fingers through it.

Then, I recited another favorite quote by Michelle Obama.

"Our first job in life as women is to get to know ourselves. I think a lot of times we don't do that. We spend our time pleasing, satisfying, looking out into the world to define who we are, listening to the messages, the images, the limited definitions that people have of who we are."

Growing through my thirties, I constantly felt like I was on a different playing field than others. It wasn't that I felt behind as I watched people get married and have kids. Ironically, I felt ahead of them. I'd seen too many of my old classmates on Facebook posting smiling pictures with their rings as they got engaged to people they'd known for just a few months or men they'd accidentally gotten pregnant with. Didn't they know that the divorce rate was almost fifty percent? I'd always known that I wanted to get married eventually, but when I did get married, I wanted it to be right, and I wanted it to last.

My fourth glass finished the bottle because of my heavy-handed pouring. I was so surprised at how quickly the bottle emptied that I instinctively looked around my living room as if I had guests that were sharing the bottle with me. When my now-drunk mind remembered I was home alone, I laughed to myself, which echoed in the empty townhouse. The wine was most certainly hitting me now. Perhaps finishing a whole bottle in thirty minutes was not the most ingenious idea, but what was the harm if I was already home with no intentions of going out anymore?

I closed my eyes and firmly reminded myself as if I was giving a pep talk, "Being single used to mean that nobody wanted you. Now it meant you were pretty, sexy, and taking your time deciding how you want your life to be and who you want to spend it with." Most recently, this Carrie Bradshaw quote was my new favorite. However, it wasn't until that moment, as I sat in my moonlit living room, feeling a little bit more than tipsy, that I fully realized why I was so drawn to this quote around my fortieth birthday.

Because I had been focused only on bettering myself and furthering my career, I subconsciously thought that I had an endless supply of time to figure out the rest. Until today, I honestly did feel like I had all the time in the world. Yet somehow, when the clock struck midnight, it shattered all of my confidence, as if the slow-moving hourglass of time had broken and the sand was spilling out between my fingers.

Despite my best efforts to quiet it, my drunken mind now asked the same question I had often repeated on many a lonely night, "Ava Amore, are you sure this is worth it?"

However, for the very first time in my life, I hesitated. For the very first time, I wasn't sure if all the time, the energy, and the relationships I'd so easily given up without a "fight" were worth it. After all, here I was, sitting alone in the dark on my fortieth birthday.

Shit! I needed my playlist.

SCAN TO HEAR PLAYLIST

Unwoke & Insecure

I groaned and clawed my hand against my eyes, tired in frustration. This was never the person I intended to be. This wasn't the plan I had for myself—though, I didn't have plans to be single this long either, but I was never going to dwell on that.

I checked my Apple watch and somehow three hours had passed, unbeknownst to me. It read 11:58 PM. There were only two minutes left of this terrible birthday. Although two minutes weren't going to suddenly fix my mid-life crisis, it secretly still made me feel better that there was hope, and today was nothing more than a fluke. Like I'd gotten a twenty-four-hour bug and would return to normal tomorrow.

Nodding to myself, I did my best to reaffirm this idea, cementing the belief that it was no more than an error in a code. Taking a deep inhale through my nose then slowly exhaling out through my mouth, like my yoga instructor had taught me at the beginning and end of my yoga classes, I began to feel the knot between my shoulder blades loosen. The breathing tipped me back away from the edge, avoiding a topple into my rabbit hole of despair.

"Today is just an ordinary day," I reminded myself as I breathed. In. Out.

"I am a successful managing partner of a marketing firm and a thriving entrepreneur," I continued. In. Out.

"I have great friends and family. I live a healthy and active lifestyle, and I am a beautiful person inside and out." In. Out.

As I hyped myself up to the confidence level I used to be at, I began to feel my body release the mounting tension and the weight in my chest abate. That was the real me. The woman who always had her head held high and paid no mind to what anyone thought of her. I checked my watch again, the time read 12:05 AM. It was a new day. My birthday was over. Finally.

Although the day had barely begun, I was already beginning to feel better. I got up from the couch and grabbed myself a hard seltzer from my refrigerator, as a treat. I would raise a drink to the new day. As I left my refrigerator, I heard my phone buzz against the counter.

I tried to wrack my inebriated brain as to who would possibly be calling me at this late hour, but I could think of no one. I picked up my phone and squinted to read the caller ID. The moment my eyes focused and the name "Don" swam into view, my heart stopped. Why was Don calling me at midnight?

Of all the men I had dated in the past, Don had been a standout experience—but for all the wrong reasons. He was a gorgeous, salt-and-pepper stud I'd matched with on a dating app called Bumble. It was my first time using any kind of digital app dating, so I had no expectations of what it would be like. Based on his profile, everything about Don was perfect for me. He was handsome, successful, and career-oriented like me, so he was an instant swipe right. Later when we met up, I found out he didn't have any kids, and some time after, I learned the sex was good... really good. What wasn't there to like, right?

The rhythm of my heart started to pick up the longer I reminisced on our time spent between the eight-hundred-thread-count-sheets. The phone continued to vibrate in my hand, but I couldn't bring myself to either decline or answer. Then my mind jumped, for a moment, to our first date.

One fateful night ten months ago, I was at the office working late for an extremely important proposal when my phone chimed with a notification from Bumble. I had just set up my profile the night before and had swiped right on a few contenders in the morning before I left for work. I'd gotten a few matches and a few "heys" from men, but this was the first time getting into a conversation like this.

Hey, it's Don. Just wanted to say hello and get to know you.

I stared at my phone in disbelief that someone had finally sent me a full sentence. His confidence intrigued me, so I decided to play along and began drafting my text back to him.

Nice to meet you, Don. So, what exactly do you want to know about me?

I sent the message without thinking twice. I was confident, and at my age, I didn't have the time or patience to send screenshots to my friends and ask for their advice on what to say back, as I so often had in my twenties.

As soon as I put my phone down to return to my proposal, my phone sounded off a second time. I was a little surprised. Although I thought it was childish to play the game of waiting for a certain amount of time before responding, it was something I'd seen multiple men my age still do. To see that Don didn't care about those absurd dating rituals made me even more interested in what he had to say.

Everything. How about you tell me all about yourself tomorrow night at 7 PM?

I flushed ever so slightly at his assertiveness. Even though I had no idea who this man was beyond his dating profile, I was still interested enough from his text messages to go out on a limb.

It's a date.

I hit send and put my phone away in my drawer to avoid any more distractions from work. For the first time in a while, I was excited about a man.

The next day, he texted me good morning, and throughout the day. It was a foreign feeling talking to someone new who was so responsive and communicative. Everything about Don sounded better and better the more the day went on. When work ended at six PM, I was one of the first to leave the office and hurried home to get ready for my date. I touched up my makeup and slipped into a casual but form-fitting black dress and comfortable heels. After my twenties, as a general rule of mine, I no longer allowed my dates to pick me up from my home to avoid giving out my address and compromising my safety, so I grabbed my car keys and drove myself to our meeting spot.

Don picked a slightly upscale sushi restaurant downtown after I told him about my salmon sashimi obsession. A green flag that he was listening to me! Funnily enough, it was a restaurant I'd been dying to try for months. As I stepped out of my car and handed the valet my keys, I looked around for Don. The only thing he told me was that he had grown a beard since his photos and was wearing a navy-blue button-up shirt. As I approached the sidewalk, a tall, dark man appeared by my side with a wide grin.

"Ava?" His deep voice took me by surprise in the best way possible.

"Hello," I replied, matching his smile. "Yes, I'm Ava. And that must make you Don?" I asked playfully.

"Guilty," he said with a wink, "Perfect timing, our table is ready."

He guided me toward the restaurant and opened the door. Inside, our server directed us to a small booth tucked away in a quiet corner. I was pleased with that. I always found it too distracting and difficult to get to know someone when it sounded like a house party was going on beside me. We scooted into the booth and sat across from each other as the server placed our menus on the table. The restaurant was upscale, known for its extremely fresh fish and unique signature rolls. My mouth began to water as I browsed the menu.

Out of the corner of my eye, I could see that Don wasn't looking at the menu at all. He was staring at me with a satisfied half-smirk playing at the corners of his full lips. I blushed and averted my gaze to the menu shyly. It wasn't often I felt tongue-tied, but something about his unwavering gaze made me uncharacteristically nervous.

When the server returned ten minutes later, I ordered a chef's sashimi plate and a couple of signature rolls, expecting to share with Don. To my surprise though, he ordered a bowl of ramen and a side of shrimp tempura. The moment the server walked away, I couldn't resist asking him why.

"You don't want any sushi?" I questioned as he took a sip of his cocktail, and that playful smirk flickered across his lips again.

"No, I actually don't like sushi," he remarked casually.

"But you picked this place?" I tilted my head in confusion as I tried to make sense of things.

"Well, you mentioned you loved sushi, so..." He trailed off but lifted his glass for a toast. I brought mine up and we clinked the rims together. "To you. And sushi." I giggled and sipped the sparkling cucumber beverage, savoring the taste.

"That's... actually very sweet of you. Thank you." I reached my hand across the table and squeezed his forearm. Just a small gesture, but I felt the energy crackle between our skin. His smirk turned into a full-on grin.

"So, did I meet your expectations?" he asked, stroking his beard.

"Truthfully?" I asked, pausing for dramatic effect. "You exceeded them," I finally confessed, then turned away bashfully, surprised by how honest the words were.

"You've exceeded mine as well," Don replied quickly. "I can't imagine why a woman like you would be single. Not that I'm complaining, by any means, but I am curious."

"I haven't found the one," I said with a shrug, flicking a strand of hair away from my face and looking hard into Don's steely eyes.

"You've been hurt before?" Don's voice inquired hesitantly.

I was momentarily taken back by his comment. I chuckled nervously and thought for a moment before saying, "Thankfully, I've only had one really terrible guy in my life. The rest just... didn't work out. What about yourself?"

Forthcoming as could be, Don explained the last ten years of his dating history in a single breath. Something about his transparency made me giggle for some reason. I stared into his deep, beautiful, hazel eyes and wondered if I would be able to fall in love with this man. Studying his face carefully, I noticed how infrequently he blinked. He was so intense, it made me breathless. It distracted me from his speaking for a few minutes before I suddenly realized I wasn't blinking either. Having been gazing so hard at him, I felt my eyes water. Don paused, noticing.

"Are you crying?" he asked, his brows furrowed. He tried to offer me his napkin with sincere concern, but I waved him away.

"No, my eyes are just dry. How, um, are your eyes?" I tried to ask casually but the words sounded clunky and caused me to blush.

"Fine?" he replied with a curious look. "You're very interesting, Ava," he teased. I bit my tongue to control my expression, not wanting to portray the rollercoaster of emotions I was experiencing inside.

Though Don definitely brought out a strange, nervous side of me with his intense, unflinching honesty, he was thoughtful and surprisingly sweet. Normally, I had extremely low expectations for first dates, but my dinner with Don was one of the best evenings I'd had with a man. Certainly the best date I'd had since narcissistic, psychopathic lying-ass Larry. And prior to Larry, it had been a very long time. Maybe my policy was becoming too lax... or perhaps he was actually a serious contender for something more? We spent the rest of the meal teasing each other playfully while I finished every last piece of sushi.

At the end of our date, Don paid for dinner, helped me pick up my keys from the valet, and walked me to my car. As we stood outside my driver's side door, I could see gears turning in his head, so I waited for him to make his play.

"When can I see you again?" Don finally asked after a long pause.

"I'm free next Saturday," I remarked sweetly.

"Perfect." He flashed me another bright grin before turning around and walking away toward his car. I was a little surprised. I'd half expected him to kiss me, but then again, it was still just a first date, so I needed to keep my expectations casual. As I got into my car, I suddenly realized I was smiling. Smiling bigger than I had in a very long time.

We had another date the next Saturday. Then, the Saturday after that. Don and I continued to see each other for another four months, most of which were really good, but that was before the magic faded as the Don I met on our first date started to fizzle out. It was as if he was a coin with two vastly different sides to him. One side was extremely gentlemanly and confident, like the Don I went on a first date with. The other was ignorant and infuriating, stubborn to a fault. That was the Don I ended up dating for the last two months of our relationship. When it was good, it was great, but when it was bad, it was terrible.

The last straw finally broke me when I was at my weekly hair appointment. As a proud Black woman, I was quite comfortable with who I was and the beautiful features that I had been given. However, that didn't mean there weren't lines that shouldn't have been crossed when it came to female Black beauty.

After a long day of work, I plopped into a salon chair with my regular stylist for my weekly touchup. Being at the salon was like I was back in my childhood home with my mother and sisters making jokes and running around with their chaotic energy while they did each other's hair. The bustle put me at ease and allowed me to take my mind off my work and the week's stress. As I waited in my chair while my stylist prepped her supplies, my phone rang out with a new text message. It was Don.

Hey, Ava, I miss you.

Reading his text made me blush, even at thirty-nine years old. I felt myself soften.

I miss you too, Don. Up to anything fun?

No. What about you?

I'm at the salon right now getting my hair done. I'm thinking of changing my style.

When my phone sounded off again, my eyes immediately widened as I read his next message.

What does your natural hair look like? I'm curious what it looks like under the fake hair. Why do Black women wear fake hair?

I swallowed down hard as I thought over what I wanted to say. This wasn't the first time he'd asked a touchy question. It was always in the way he asked or said it that grated at me. Don had no decorum. So many nights I had thought about telling him off for lacking good judgment, but I always held back because a tiny part of me was still willing to cut him some slack. Don hadn't grown up in a predominately Black community, in fact, he grew up in a community with not much of a Black presence at all. Even though both his parents were Black, I felt like he still had questions about his own racial identity. However, asking me tactless questions certainly wasn't the way to learn. I felt my mood immediately sour.

My hair was shoulder length and very fine and I preferred to wear weaves for extra oomph. I looked at myself in the mirror, thinking for a moment. Then, I sent him a video of my hair from a previous appointment, before my current weave was installed. As I waited for a response my irritation mounted. I wasn't upset that he'd asked me about my weave, but the way he asked me rubbed me the wrong way, as if he was judging me for having "fake hair." It was questions like these that made me skeptical about a future with Don. I felt the heat rising up to my throat as I continued to stare at the text message in disappointment. I was waiting for a response, yet I was still nervous about what he would say. Had he asked any of his exes that question?

Thinking back, he'd told me that he only had experience dating Hispanic and White women, so I assumed the answer was no. So why did he have to specifically ask me, as if Black women who wore weaves automatically had no hair or "bad hair?"

The next day I woke up, still put off from Don's question about my hair. I thought about all the comments he'd made in the past, and it blew my mind how culturally ignorant he really was. Not to mention, he hadn't even bothered to respond to my last message. I sighed, frustrated enough to cut my losses then and there, but in order to be absolutely fair, I tried one last time to give him the benefit of the doubt. It was technically possible I'd misinterpreted his tone.

For the first time in a long time, I felt the need for a second opinion. Feeling validated, though a little juvenile, I snapped a screenshot and fired it off to my group chat of best friends to see what they had to say about the situation. Instantly, a bombardment of texts came flooding in.

Sidney, Nina, and Hannah were all extremely adamant about me leaving Don alone for good. Although they had only met a handful of times, they each had their qualms about him, and it was a unanimous vote for good riddance.

Sidney had been the first to talk to me after the first few dinners we'd had together with Don. He was nice and cordial but still made some "interesting" comments about how he would never allow the girl he was dating to go to the club or a bar without him. However, Sidney being the no BS type of girl she was, could not sit back and hold her tongue. As soon as dinner was over and we were walking to the parking lot, she pulled me into the bathroom to tell me straight up how she felt about Don.

"Listen, I'm just saying you should keep an eye out for jealous behavior like that. It's a red flag," she whispered to me as we washed our hands in front of a row of mirrors that reflected her wary face six times over.

It was quite an earful, per usual, but she wasn't wrong. Truthfully, it made me a little uncomfortable at how much he didn't trust women in general. Naturally, it made me wonder if he didn't trust me either. Still, Sidney didn't often like the people any of us dated, and Don was no exception, so it made it easy enough to brush her concerns off. That was, until another friend came to me with more concerns.

The next to speak up was Hannah, after meeting Don for the third time. We were at my townhouse having a daytime barbecue, sharing recipes and avidly discussing how we each seasoned and marinated the dishes that we'd brought. In the natural lull of the conversation around the table while people ate, Hannah's at-the-time boyfriend asked Don if he wanted to help cook the next round of ribs. Don adamantly refused. Even though the ribs only needed heating up, Don was too afraid of messing up and potentially ruining the barbecue. When the boyfriend pushed back, Don snapped at him.

"I'm not a man who goes back on my word. Especially when that word is no," he argued sternly. The table was silent for a moment before Hannah coughed uncomfortably and offered to do it herself.

At the time, I didn't see a problem with him not wanting to burn the food, but Hannah texted me later that night about how Don made a mountain out of a molehill. She clarified her boyfriend was simply asking to get to know Don better, not putting unwanted responsibility on his shoulders. There was no need for him to be rude. I apologized on his behalf, though unfortunately this was not for the last time.

Finally, Nina came to me after meeting Don for the fifth time at a dinner party at her house. It was supposed to be a nice, casual taco and beer night when Don had to yet again make everyone uncomfortable. After a delicious and peaceful dinner, Nina brought out Mexican fruit cups seasoned with chamoy and tajin as dessert. My mouth was already watering at the sight of pineapple and mango, but as I reached out to grab one, Don stopped me gently.

"Don't worry babe, I'll get it for you. Which do you want?" he offered. Leeta made a tiny oh sound and batted her eyes in support of my relationship. I shot her a wink.

"Any is fine. They all look delicious!" I giggled like a little schoolgirl at Don taking care of me.

"No, I don't like that," he replied, his smile slipping, slightly fading." I want you to tell me which one you want."

"It really doesn't matter, Don. It's just fruit." I shrugged my shoulders and tried to laugh it off, but Don's face was completely serious.

"It matters to me. I don't want to give you something you don't like and then you get upset with me later," he explained firmly, which caught everyone's attention at the table. "It's important to me that you can be decisive. I can't make all the choices for you."

I immediately began to seethe. I was perfectly capable of making choices and he knew damn well that was the case. I could feel everyone's eyes on us, which made the entire situation extremely awkward as I tried to will away the flush in my cheeks.

"When have I ever gotten upset with you over something like that?" I hissed, trying my best to stay calm. I could feel all the eyes at the table boring into me, so I dropped my gaze and bit my lip to avoid saying anything I was going to regret. Don seemed to pick up on my discomfort because he didn't reply. The last thing I wanted to do was have a fight in front of my best friends and their significant others, so I gave in and changed the topic.

"I like pineapple," I told him politely as I forced a smile and stood up to grab a piece myself. After dessert, we moved to the living room to watch a movie together, but as I sat down beside Don, Nina called me over for help to clean up the kitchen. Leaving Don behind with everyone else, Nina and I started to pack up the leftover food and clear the dishes to run in the dishwasher. Nina looked over her shoulder to make sure no one was coming over.

"Okay, so that whole fruit situation was weird, right?" She asked me under her breath. I contemplated for a moment whether or not I was ready to get into that incident with Nina.

I knew everything always needed to be exactly the way she wanted it. She had always been incredibly inflexible to things and people outside her comfort zone. She would have hated it if her partner did something like that to her in front of friends.

"Yes, but—" I started, when she cut me off.

"But what? Why was it such a big deal to pick the wrong fruit? It's not like you were allergic to anything!" she whispered so loudly it was barely a whisper anymore.

"He just gets like that sometimes." I shook my head as I continued to rinse her dishes. I felt angry that I was forced to defend him, even while I was still fuming inside.

"I know I gave my blessing when you first showed me his profile, but I don't know about that decision anymore. He seemed so nice based on his bio, but every time I talk to him, I get weird vibes." Nina shuddered a little to herself as if she had seen a spider. I suddenly felt embarrassed. I had to admit that Don definitely had his moments when he was not the best company or the most well-spoken in the room. It didn't mean he was some kind of creep though, because there were still many times I enjoyed being around him.

"At the end of the day he's a good guy, but he's far from perfect. He has an incredibly narrow mind and uncomfortably loose tongue," I began to explain when Nina interrupted me again.

"And you're okay with that?" she retorted, causing me to pause and ponder her question. My silence must have spoken volumes to Nina. "I don't know if he's right for you, Ava," Nina concluded as she put down the dishes and looked at me with concerned eyes. I knew her worries were coming from a good place, but I still didn't feel like his flaws were as bad as she was saying they were. Was I deluding myself? Or were my friends blind to the good in him?

"I don't know. He's not all bad," I said as I leaned against the sink and groaned. At this point, I was beginning to wonder if I was convincing Nina or myself.

"But do you see a future?" Nina repeated firmly with her maternal instincts kicking in.

"I really don't know." I threw my hands in the air and sent splashes of water all over the sink and counter. The only person who didn't tell me that I needed to break up with Don was Leeta, which was expected since she didn't have a single hateful bone in her body. No matter how many times she felt uncomfortable or didn't sit well with something he said, she always kept a smile on her face and gave a positive spin to the conversation to alleviate some of the awkward tension. I was grateful that at least one person was supportive of my relationship, but Leeta was notorious for dating the worst men, so having her on my side was truthfully bittersweet at best.

Almost all of my friends continued to tell me I deserved better. At the root of it all, they agreed that Don's problems boiled down to deep-rooted insecurity. From the way he was deathly afraid of being cheated on to his irrational fear of being wrong and causing a fight, Don's flaws all came from a good place but were so misguided that they, in turn, began to cause even bigger problems. The cracks started to show.

Despite his first impression of being a proud and confident person, the facade melted away like ice cream in July, leaving only a soggy waffle cone behind. When we were younger, it was much easier to accept our friends dating slightly problematic people, however, now that we were all almost in our forties, my friends had lost their patience for men who weren't going to be in a lasting relationship with us. I did take what they said into consideration when I thought about my relationship with Don, but for me, there was something that made it hard for me to let him go.

I tried to tell myself that maybe if I was more understanding and patient with him, he would learn to become more sure of himself. So, instead of dwelling on his flaws, I decided to become more supportive. I treated him like the Don I met on our first date, in hopes he might transform into that man again. The Don who picked a restaurant with food he didn't eat because I said I liked it. The Don who took the initiative to ask me out on a second date while we were still on our first. The Don who stared at me unwaveringly and unflinchingly, who made me feel seen and special for the first time in a long time. I wanted that Don back and there was still hope deep down inside of me that the person I first had feelings for was still there.

One night we were at his apartment having cocktails. I was drinking a fourth Aperol spritz and he was having an IPA when I drunkenly asked him why he was so afraid of getting things wrong or potentially making me upset.

He paused at my question and quietly sipped on his beer as he pondered how to navigate explaining his feelings. As I waited for his response, I could sense that this was something he wanted to talk about and suddenly realized no one had ever asked him before.

Finally, after a long silence, he finished the last of his beer, leaned closer to me, and gently grabbed my hands. He confessed that it was much easier for him to lower his walls down on our first date because he had nothing to lose. Meeting a beautiful girl for the first time was easy, he said. But the longer we dated, the more he became worried about not being good enough, or worse, losing me to another man. The conversation resulted in a lot of tears and earnest worries, which made me even more sympathetic to him than before. I really appreciated how willing he was to talk about his feelings and let me into his most vulnerable thoughts.

For the next two months, we both continued to try and make things work. For a moment there was a glimmer of hope that night as he held my hands and gazed into my soul with shining eyes. Still, no matter how hard either of us tried, I couldn't get past my own discomfort in our relationship. Those words, those truths, were beautiful, but they could only carry us so far.

In the end, I didn't care that he wasn't as confident as he pretended to be, or even that he was constantly worried about losing me to another man. It wasn't any of the comments from my best friends and their skepticism about him being a good fit for me either. After six months of emotional turmoil, his inability to properly understand me as a Black woman was what eventually pushed me to break up with him. Though I hated to admit it, after the salon incident, nothing between Don and I was ever the same.

My phone stopped ringing, and I was suddenly brought back to reality from the flood of memories. I shook my swimming head, trying to clear it of the racing thoughts that clouded my ability to see. It was like coming up for air after swimming underwater for hours.

I didn't expect to be so distracted with my thoughts that the call ended before I could answer it. Although I was slightly curious as to why he was calling me in the first place, the moment I remembered how socially inept he was toward Black women, I was disgusted with him all over again. There was absolutely no chance I would ever consider getting back with Don, even if someone paid me a million dollars. I had ignored all of the advice from my friends and even the red flags I noticed myself in order to become the person who could best support Don and help him become the man I knew he once was again. But reality didn't work that way, and it took having to put my feelings aside to make me finally see that there was nothing that was going to make Don into the man I hoped he was. No one is perfect. I'm not searching for perfection, as the Lord knows

I'm nowhere near it, but overwhelming insecurities and cultural ignorance, especially from a Black man, was where I drew the line.

I left my phone on the counter as I padded back to my couch and took a seat. Being alone, even on a night like tonight, was better than being with him, I reminded myself.

Shit! I needed a drink and my playlist.

SCAN TO HEAR PLAYLIST

WOKE (Drink Recipe)
Mexican Green Tea

Materials needed: shaking tin w/top, ice, Sprite, and sour mix
Alcohol needed: tequila (Casimigos) preferably silver, peach schnapps (Dekuyper)
Grab shaker tin fill w/ ice and add:
4 count(2oz) tequila
2 count (1oz) peach schnapps
1 count (.5 oz) sour mix
Shake it, pour in glass and top with 1 count (.5oz) of Sprite

Good Trouble

Halfway through my drink, I found myself scrolling through the pictures on my phone. I gently laid my head back and smiled. I stumbled upon "Good Trouble,"—at least that's what I called him the first day we met. Rick was a man with a solid, chiseled build of a six-foot-one Adonis and the most beautiful smile you've ever seen. That smile just had a special way of warming my heart that made me forget all of my worries. But don't let that sweet grin deceive you, he was a ladies' man.

The first time we met, we enjoyed each other's conversation over a cup of hot tea and a cinnamon crumb cake, dining at a Starbucks, situated midway between our homes. He had tea, and I had tea and a crumb cake. It's something about Starbucks' crumb cake that's hard for me to resist.

We found a table in the corner and sat across from each other, which gave me a full view of Rick's very handsome face. As he spoke, I found myself lost in his eyes. Rick was a full-eye-contact kind of guy, another factor that made it hard to focus on his words.

As we sat and talked, I kept telling myself, don't be a whore, don't be a whore, Ava. There was just something about this man I couldn't quite understand that made me so instantly drawn to him. We were both dressed casually, both in jeans and a t-shirt since we made a snap decision to meet at the last minute. This was supposed to be a low-stakes coffee meetup. I wasn't even sure if I would have considered it a date! So, it wasn't like he had on his Saturday night's best, but yet, I still felt those sparks—sexual sparks, that is. Undeniable chemistry. This was our first time seeing each other in person, and boy did Rick make an impression on me.

We spent about an hour talking, and everything was going great. Rick and I covered a lot of the typical small talk topics and the conversation flowed effortlessly. I found myself smiling and laughing harder than usual at things that weren't even really that funny. We lingered over our empty cups for a while before finally getting up and heading back to our cars. Like a gentleman, Rick kept me close by his side as we walked through the parking lot, holding my arm with the softest touch. As we approached my car, he gently grabbed me by my waist to pull me a little closer to him. I said to myself, *Lord, please control these raging hormones.* Just the slightest touch from him was enough to make my whole-body quiver.

Right before I got in the car, he again pulled me tight against him and gave me an innocent kiss on the lips. He tasted like green tea, which was a perfect complement to my crumb cake. I melted. As he pulled away, I wanted so badly to hold onto him longer and savor the moment but instead was left aching for another taste. I turned away to hide my flushed cheeks. I couldn't let him see me blush like a schoolgirl having her first kiss. After we bid each other goodbye and he walked away, I got in the car, started it, and sat back in the seat, too jelly-kneed to drive, with a big goofy grin across my face. I was warm all over and far too excited to keep the excitement to myself.

Still feeling high, I decided to call one of my best friends to gush about my meeting with Rick. Before even making it to the freeway, I commanded, "Siri, call Sidney."

"Calling Sidney," Siri replied over my car speakers.

As the dial tone rang. I couldn't keep my fingers still on the steering wheel as I drove. I was too electrified by the excitement from Rick to contain myself. I had to tell someone about it.

"Hello?" Sidney answered after a handful of rings.

"Sidney! I have to tell you about this date. It was a dream," I started as soon as I heard her voice.

"Oh, um, yeah, that's great! Tell me all about it," she replied unenthusiastically. I could tell that something in her voice was different, but I couldn't put my finger on what. However, I was too distracted to take the time and figure it out.

"His name is Rick. I think I showed you a picture when we got drinks last week. It's crazy, I know I just met him, but he makes me feel all funny inside. But in a good way, of course, like a goofy teenager." I stopped to sigh heavily as a picture of Rick sitting across from me at Starbucks flashed through my mind, only in my imagination he was shirtless and wearing grey sweatpants.

"He's just so... sexy."

"Dang, girl, it sounds like you found a good one," Sidney laughed.

"I hope so! I guess we'll see. I have to say though, I envy you. No more second-guessing or worrying about where things are going," I confessed, a bit embarrassed. There was no shame in being older and single, but I did have my days when I craved the comfort and stability my married friends had, although admitting it was rare.

"Yeah, I guess you could say that," Sidney replied

unconvincingly. This time, her tone registered more clearly to me.

"What do you mean? Of course, that's what it is. It's marriage," I replied, confused by what underlying message Sidney was trying to communicate. As I continued driving, I heard some muffled noises from the other end of the line, then a door shut.

Sidney dropped her voice into a quiet whisper.

"I can't really talk right now, but I really need to speak with you later. I'll call you back another time?"

"Yeah, definitely. Are you sure you're okay?" I questioned hesitantly.

"Great, talk to you then. Bye," then, Sidney hung up on me before answering my last question, though, judging by her tone, I had my answer.

Her cryptic words were concerning, but until she told me what was going on, there was nothing I could do except wait for her to call me back. So in order to keep my mind off the mystery, I redirected my full attention to the road. However, it only took a few minutes of driving for my mind to slip back into a dizzying daze of Rick again.

Over the next few weeks, Rick and I kept in touch, but barely. We only texted each other casually a handful of times, but it wasn't something that I took to heart. It was the holiday

season, after all. We were both with our families, and since we weren't anything serious, there wasn't any expectation to frequently contact each other. So we kept things low-pressure and just texted the casual Merry Christmas, Happy New Year, and "how are you?"

About a week into the New Year, as I was enjoying a cup of coffee on the couch, my phone rang, and to my surprise, it was Rick. I answered the call, trying to downplay my excitement, and we exchanged flirtatious pleasantries. He told me about a few crazy family stories over the holidays and I told him mine. It was nice to finally bond with someone over the little things.

As we were laughing over the phone, the conversation took an unexpected turn when he told me, "I want to reward you for your patience."

"My patience?" I asked.

"Yes, thank you for being so patient over the last few weeks. I had a lot going on with family and work, so, again, I want to reward you for your patience," he repeated plainly.

I laughed to myself, ignoring the fact that he could hear me on the other end. Who said I was patiently waiting? But I had to admit, I was a little bit intrigued about the "reward" he wanted to give to me. Hell, who was I fooling, I was a lot intrigued! I could almost see his beautiful smile through the phone. And he made me laugh. A man that can keep me laughing is a keeper in my book. *Fuck it,* I thought, *go get that reward. Live a little. You deserve it.*

"I suppose I have been rather patient…"

The interesting thing about Rick was that he didn't find the need to "lie to kick it," as he'd put it. He was one of those brutally honest people. Sometimes too honest. He was the type of person who let you know exactly what he wanted, and he wouldn't lead you on unintentionally. Rick was going to do Rick, and if he could do you in the process, that was a bonus. After enough failed relationships, it made me appreciate his candor even more. He was a breath of fresh air from previously dealing with lying-ass Larry, though that mess was a story for another day.

I appreciated a man who showed up as himself and found no need to be presentational. During this day and age, that was sexy as hell and very rare. I knew what I was getting into with "Good Trouble." Hell, I'm grown. He's grown. He came right on time. Rick wasn't only what I wanted, but what I needed at that moment. There was something about him that made me feel comfortable and protected. I didn't trust easily, so I had never felt that way for any man so soon. But with Rick, I let my guard way down. It felt right—or so I thought.

We continued to text back and forth. At one point, he even sent me a couple of steamy pictures, showing off all that he had to offer if you know what I mean. My eyes traveled down his barrel chest and washboard abs, then landed on his fitted boxers. I felt my cheeks flush as I noticed what clearly was a dick imprint. No way. It can't be. He's not even erect. I smirked and bit my lip. He undeniably seemed to have all the equipment in all the right places. I was definitely more curious now.

Rick and I had also done some serious shit talking to one another, teasing each other playfully back and forth. I was excited and ready for it—again, so I thought. Little did I know, Rick was about to make me eat every shit-talkin' word I had said.

The next day, after the sexy picture had been sent, he called and asked me to come over. His exact instructions were to "wear something sexy and bring my overnight bag." After where my mind went when he sent me that photo, I was quick to oblige. However, by nightfall when it was time for me to get ready to leave, I was in no mood to squeeze into a tight dress or snap on a pair of high heels. It had been a long exhausting day and I was actually getting really sleepy.

However, this opportunity with Rick was not something I was

going to throw away lightly. I convinced myself to jump in the shower, lotion up, and grab my black satin Victoria Secret's robe out of the drawer. Wearing just a pair of black lace panties underneath, I threw some clothes in a bag, slid on my silver studded sandals, and walked out the door. No bra, no pants, just a robe and panties. Sexy enough?

It was going to take me about twenty-five minutes to get to his condo. It only took me five before I began to rethink my outfit choice. The entire rest of the ride, I kept asking myself, *Ava, what in the world are you doing? You don't know this man. You only met him in person one time, spoke with him for less than an hour, and now you're about to show up to this man's condo half naked with no real clue what you're about to walk into!* Exhaling sharply, I looked up toward the sky at a red light to pray that I wasn't making a huge mistake.

"Lord, I know you're tired of my shenanigans, but please watch over me tonight and get me back home safely."

Can you even pray while sinning all at the same time? Praying to be blessed in sin. I don't know, but it was worth a shot.

For some reason, I couldn't bring myself to turn around, and the next thing I knew, I was at his parking garage waiting for the gate to open. *Lord, I know I need to get back into church and can't go this weekend, but I'll look into it next week. Amen.*

With other cars in front and behind me, I pulled into this well-lit parking structure and left the car in his reserved spot. Looking around at the bright lights, I started to feel embarrassed and incredibly self-conscious about my cheeky outfit. I hadn't thought much about the practical aspects of walking upstairs practically naked, with strangers to the left and right of me. Those other people were probably not paying attention to me, but when you're doing skanky shit, it feels like the whole world is watching your stupidity in action.

Rick met me at the bottom of the staircase by the parking structure and looked me up and down before saying, "Shall we?"

A devilish smile crept across his face as he gestured up the steps.

I followed behind him closely and held down the bottom of my robe to avoid flashing anyone below. Luckily, he lived on the second floor, close to the parking structure, so I was able to slip inside without prying eyes taking a peek. After two minutes of walking, once inside, I made myself comfortable on the couch. He joined me, sitting close, with our knees brushing up against each other and his hand on my thigh.

I laughed at just about everything he said, even though he wasn't that damn funny. I was simply in such a state of anxious excitement that the only way to calm my nerves a bit was for me to laugh. It had been a long time since I had butterflies.

He made me a nice little drink, which wasn't too strong, but for someone who had only eaten a Wetzel Pretzel the whole day, a couple of sips had my head spinning. It felt like an out-of-body experience, sitting drizzly beside him as I inhaled the spicy scent of his cologne, and I quickly felt embarrassed. I thought to myself, *Ava, you're too old to be twisted off a couple of sips. Get your shit together and act like the grown ass woman you are.*

It was too late though, I caught myself giggling like a schoolgirl, and had already completely embarrassed myself, so I thought.

We talked, listened to music, and watched a little TV—casual date night stuff. We moved closer and he wrapped his arm around me as we half-watched the movie on the screen. I nestled closer and he gave me a lascivious smile.

The next thing I knew, he had pulled his manhood out of his shorts. I stifled a gasp. It was a bold move, but that wasn't what really took me back. It was the size. It went up his stomach and damn near to his chest. I felt my eyes go wide.

"Is your di–"

Before I could get the words out, he said, "Shhhhhh."

He knew what I was about to ask. Quite frankly, I was speechless. What in the world did I just witness? I had never in my life seen a penis that big, at least not in person. The closest I had ever come to one that big was while watching Pornhub or XNXX. A mix of emotions and sensations flooded my body and mind. I was excited, nervous, enamored, and fascinated all at the same time. It all felt new, and, in my mind, I was screaming, *Siri, play 'Like a Virgin' by Madonna on Tidal.*

He took my hand and led me to the king-sized bed inside his master suite. I laid down and batted my eyes up at him, holding my breath, waiting for him to make a move. A half pump in and I was damn near jumping backwards. He kneeled at the end of the bed and looked down at me, practically licking his lips.

"Ava, Ava, Ava, we talked about this. You're gonna take this dick."

I was shocked. No one had ever said anything like that to me. Once again, I embarrassed myself with another laugh. If he couldn't do anything else, he could always make me laugh. However, I soon found out that he could do something else.

Everything happened fast after that. He pinned me down with the weight of his muscular body as his fingers danced down my stomach and between my legs. I let out a soft moan of pleasure. Two minutes in, I came—0hard. Once again, I flushed with embarrassment. I thought to myself, *damn Ava, you couldn't go for at least ten minutes?*

The truth was, though, I couldn't hold back. Rick had touched every wall and completely filled the room inside of me with his incredible girth, all the way to the deepest depths of my soul. When I'd finally caught my breath, I got up, went into the bathroom, and washed away the evidence of our encounter. It was then time to go to bed. I walked back into the bedroom, and he gave me a pillow with a satin casing and said,

"Here, I even have a satin pillowcase for your hair."

I took the pillow, grinned, and shook my head. I thought to myself *if this ain't the smoothest negro I'd ever met, I didn't know who is.* He really was "Good Trouble."

Usually, I didn't sleep too well in a strange bed, and given the fact that I was sleeping with a complete stranger, I'm surprised I even drifted off at all. I slept the whole night and I slept good, like a baby. When I woke the next morning, Rick was already up doing his morning stretch routine. I crawled from the bed and gently touched his back, quietly mumbling,

"Good morning."

He gave me a kiss on the cheek before hinging over to stretch his back, and I went into the restroom to ready myself for the day. I was in a hurry to get myself together to leave.

Once he finished his morning stretch, he came out of his room and into the kitchen for a proper good morning greeting. I couldn't help myself from looking at that imprint again.

I said to myself, *Jesus, be a fence and get me out of here*. That smile, that walk, his voice, and that damn imprint—I had to go!

After I gave him a long hug goodbye, he walked me to my car, and I left without looking back. On my drive back home, I was in a daze. I laughed, yet again. I felt crazy and overwhelmed, but, ultimately, I wanted a do-over. I needed more. But I knew I had to control my emotions. After all, I was dealing with "Good Trouble," and I knew it. There was no time for fairytales. I had a career and a business to get back to. I had shit to do, but a less than twenty-four-hour fling was fun while it lasted.

For the rest of that day and the next, Rick remained on my mind. It had nothing to do with sex but everything to do with his spirit, energy, and the way he made me feel comfortable and safe. That meant more to me than he would ever know. I felt I was in the company of a pure, good, kind human. He was the kind of person you didn't easily let go or forget. Unlike most guys I had been with during my life, my attraction to Rick had nothing to do with sex, though the fact that it was good was an added bonus. In such a short time, I felt like I found and connected with a beautiful soul. Rick was going to be my friend for life, and that was much more valuable and precious to me than any intimate relationship could ever be.

Don't get me wrong, Rick was one blessed, adorable, and very talented brother. And as crazy as that evening was for me, I would never forget it for all the right reasons. I just needed to be in the arms of someone safe—even if for only one night.

We continued to talk and check on one another from time to time. Although we didn't ever have sex again, Rick eventually did become a good friend to me. I truly believed that people came into our life for a reason and some for just a season. I didn't know why, but there was certainly a reason for Rick. I genuinely cared a lot for him and his well-being. He had become my buddy for life.

The next week, after a lot of reminiscing about Rick, I was putting away my dishes from dinner when I heard my phone ring from the living room. I dried my hands and hustled to pick up my phone; Sidney's name flashed across the screen, and I quickly answered before it could go to voicemail. It'd been a few days since the last time we talked and she'd sounded really weird over the phone.

"Hey, is everything okay?" I asked right away.

"Honestly, no. That's why I wanted to talk. I wanted to tell you first 'cause I don't think I'm ready to let everyone else know…" Sidney's voice was shaking.

"Slow down, Sidney. What's going on?" I sat down to brace myself for what was to come.

"I don't have any proof yet, and it's still just a hunch but…" Her voice drifted off as she sniffled.

"Proof for what?"

"I think Alex is cheating on me," Sidney finally admitted with a completely flat tone. There was absolute silence. At that moment, I froze, Sidney froze, and even time froze. Neither of us knew what to say next now that the cat was out of the bag.

"Wha—are you sure?" I gasped as I tried to process what she had just said.

"No, not exactly, but he's been acting really strange lately. I just can't put my finger on exactly what's going on, but I can feel it, Ava,

I can feel it," Sidney urged with her voice on the verge of tears.

"Oh no," I accidentally let slip.

I knew it wasn't helpful, but I couldn't wrap my head around the shock of Sidney's news. Although all of us had our concerns about her marriage, the thought of infidelity didn't cross any of our minds –certainly not mine!

"He's been coming home later than usual. Apparently, he has these 'meetings' at night, but it doesn't make any sense. Who has meetings at night after they've already left the office?!" she ranted in frustration. I could hear the vitriol coloring her voice.

"You're right. That's definitely fishy. How long has this been going on?"

"Maybe six months? And the thing is, when he is home, things just don't feel the same anymore." Her voice dropped in defeat.

"Are you guys still having sex?" I asked gently, hoping my question didn't cross the line.

"Not really…" Sidney mumbled.

"Oh," I whispered.

"Right? That's definitely a bad sign, right?" Sidney questioned with the heaviest sigh as if she was finally facing the facts.

"I mean, sometimes I guess that can happen—"

"He only seems happy when he's on his phone, which is all the time now. I don't know what I was thinking, getting married to him so quickly…" Sidney's voice drifted off as she began to choke up. She took a moment to collect herself before finishing. "I know deep down I still love him but what if he doesn't love me anymore?"

I opened my mouth to speak but no words came out. I'd never thought of relationships that way before. Like anyone else, I'd had my ups and downs, my fair share of good and bad relationships, and had my heart broken before, but I've never been married to give experienced sound advice on what to do when you think your marriage is falling apart? I closed my mouth and tried to collect my thoughts, but no matter how many times I tried to think about what to do or say to help Sidney, I had no clue. I felt utterly useless.

"I just really don't know what to do, Ava. I don't have any proof, but my gut is really telling me that it's true. The red flags are waving right in my face." Sidney finally broke down crying, something she didn't do often. Always hiding behind her sarcastic nature, Sidney was one of the emotionally strongest people I knew. She didn't let anyone or anything get her down, no matter how much it hurt her. So to see that her marriage was on the verge of falling apart and her heart was torn into pieces like this, made my heart break. I had no game plan, no words of comfort. I was at a loss.

The tears continued to flood our call as Sidney sobbed into her phone. I sat in silence and I listened to the sound of her heart crumbling in real-time. Out of solidarity, I almost started crying too but did my best to set my emotions aside, keeping myself composed. At the very least, having two people crying wasn't going to be productive in this kind of situation.

I waited until her tears began to subside, giving her time to release the pent of feelings she'd been holding back. It hurt to know she'd felt she had to keep this huge secret to herself for months. I couldn't imagine the pain she was going through, having to bottle up this kind of stress and feel too afraid or uncomfortable to tell anyone.

"Sidney, first of all, I want you to breathe. I know that sounds super cliché, but just try to take a breath and slow down. I don't want you to fall apart because he couldn't follow through with the promises he made to you. If that's even the case. Let's just take things one step at a time and see where that takes us, okay?" I reasoned with her calmly. Sidney remained silent for a few seconds, with the exception of her ragged breathing into the receiver.

"I know that you're right, but it's just so hard..." she groaned, then sniffled again.

"It's okay. We will get to the bottom of this, and everything will be okay, with or without him," I firmly reminded her. I didn't want to explicitly say the D-word but hoped to remind her that divorce was a non-embarrassing option if he really was cheating.

"Okay, thank you, Ava. I was honestly really scared of telling anyone. You know how everyone gets. Nina would just tell me all of the things I was doing wrong as a wife, Hannah would force me to stop crying, and Leeta would end up a bigger emotional mess than me! You're the only one I could trust with this, and I'm really glad I did." Sidney's voice cleared up a bit as she spoke.

"We're gonna get through this," I reminded her.

"Thanks. I have to go now, but can we get lunch together sometime soon?" Sidney asked softly.

"Definitely!"

We hung up the phone and I headed to my bedroom where I fell backward onto my bed with the biggest sigh. Truthfully, I still couldn't wrap my head around Sidney's situation, but I couldn't let that show to her. The only thing I could do was make sure that she felt supported, validated, and empowered. Any kind of infidelity was hard, but the kind that ended in divorce was the hardest.

My blood began to boil and my sadness ebbed away the longer I thought about how undeserving her husband was in the first place. Whether or not he was actually cheating, how could he put her through this kind of emotional torment? If he was being faithful, why couldn't he just communicate to her in a way where she felt confident in him? Where he was clear and didn't leave suspicion that made his wife cry over the phone to her best friend late at night?

Leave it to a man to screw up a good thing, I thought

I released a frustrated groan and grabbed my memory foam pillow. Vengeful thoughts ran through my head like a marathon, quickly draining the last bit of energy I had left after a long day. I shimmied under my feather-down comforter and tucked myself into my California king-sized bed, my eyelids growing heavy with every passing second. Despite how tired my body was, my mind was still wide awake. Part of me was still recovering from Sidney's news and the other part of me somehow drifted back to Rick. I couldn't believe how my mind went back to him after everything I heard, but his gorgeous smile and our effortless conversation were hard to forget when my mind was tired and vulnerable. The more Rick crept into my mind, the more my thoughts drifted toward other intimate encounters that awakened more than just my brain. His muscular arms, defined abdomen, and the way he liked to play with my hair made me all fuzzy inside. My toes curled as I recalled his soft lips on my neck. I had already friend-zoned him, though it certainly didn't feel that way.

I threw my pillow over my face and released a frustrated noise, allowing the memory foam to muffle my cry. When I removed the pillow, I stared up at the ceiling and tapped my face gently to bring myself back to reality. However, even slapping my own face wasn't enough to stop my body from craving that familiar taste.

Shit! I needed a drink and my playlist.

SCAN TO HEAR PLAYLIST

BIG DICK ENERGY (Drink Recipe)
Strawberry Lemonade Martini

Materials needed: mixing tin, chilled martini glass, lemons (cut in 4s), sugar
Alcohol: Ketel 1
Nonalcoholic: sour mix, strawberry purée, simple syrup

Grab mixing tin, combine ice, 7 count (3.5 oz) Ketel 1, a dash of sour (.5oz) sour mix, 2 count (1oz) strawberry purée, squeeze 3 halves lemons, dash of simple syrup (.5oz)

Grab a plate and pour sugar on it. Grab the last half of lemon, rub it all over the rim of the glass, then take the chilled martini glass, rim down, stick it in the plate of sugar.

Shake the mixing tin, pour only liquid in the glass. Garnish with a lemon peel! Now Martinis are normally stirred not shaken, but Big Dick Energy calls for it!

Best Friends to the Rescue

When I woke up the next morning, my thoughts were in a haze with the strange mix of memories of Rick and the alarming call with Sidney. Putting aside the flashes of heat with Rick, I reached over to the nightstand for my phone to call my best friend and make sure she was okay. I honestly couldn't imagine what suspecting my husband of infidelity was like, but it had to feel heart-crushing, especially after telling someone else. If I were her, telling someone would make the feeling much more real.

As I dialed Sidney's number, I stared up at the ceiling in bed, hoping she would pick up. But the phone continued to ring until I reached an automated voice mailbox. For some reason, I had this gut feeling that something wasn't right. Perhaps it was just my paranoia getting to me, but it was as if something fishy was in the air and that fishiness was bad news. However, it was still morning, so I tried to convince myself that maybe she was just simply busy. Everyone misses a phone call every now and then, so one missed call shouldn't be something to worry about. Or at least that's what I tried to tell myself. To keep my mind off of Sidney's missed call, I scrolled through social media and current news on my phone while I waited for her to call me back. Now that it was Saturday, I didn't have work to do so I had all the time in the world to relax and hope for the best.

After half an hour of reading, I got up and started my day. Before getting out of bed, I called her a second time, hoping for a different outcome, but she still didn't pick up, so I left the phone behind in my bedroom and headed to the kitchen to cook breakfast—something I rarely ever did. There wasn't much in my kitchen because I usually ate out at restaurants, so toast and cereal were gonna have to do. I munched on my toast blankly as I stared in the direction of my bedroom, straining my ears to pick up any kind of notification sound from my phone.

"Maybe I just didn't hear her call or text me back," I told myself as I brought my breakfast to the bedroom to check on my phone.

However, there were no new notifications. I ate my breakfast in silence, telling myself that I had to wait at least another thirty minutes before calling her a third time. The intuition in my gut was doing cartwheels in my stomach to get my attention, but my mind was telling me to slow down and hold off of doing anything rash. I chewed my toast slowly in an attempt to calm myself down, but my anxiety was too stressed by Sidney's absence. Although we were all busy with different schedules, this didn't sound like Sidney at all. She was the type of person who at least sent back a text saying she'd call back later if she didn't have time to answer my call, so this radio silence was not like her. As soon as the clock marked thirty minutes, I whipped around to snatch my phone so quickly it nearly flew out of my hand. I dialed her number at lightning speed and anxiously waited for her to answer. Low and behold, I reached her voicemail for a third time. One missed call was not a problem, but three in a single morning was.

"I can't sit here anymore. I gotta do something about this," I told myself as I threw my phone onto the bed and rushed to my closet to get ready.

I quickly changed into leggings and a sweater before grabbing my car keys. Leaving the dishes from breakfast in my bedroom, I dashed out the front door with a fire in my chest that only continued to burn brighter the longer Sidney didn't answer my call. I wouldn't have been this worried any other day, but after the news she broke to me last night and how shaky she sounded on the phone, I just needed absolute confirmation that she was okay. I jumped into my car and pulled out of my parking spot without any hesitation. This state of mind was one of the worst to be driving under, but a woman had no choice when her best friend's well-being was at stake!

Luckily, Sidney's home was only twenty-five minutes away from mine, so I arrived safely in good time. Had it been Leeta's house, I would have gone insane for forty minutes, being a maniac on the road. But since Sidney lived nearby, I obeyed all the traffic laws and did a full stop at every red light and stop sign, despite my heart telling me to go faster and just run them. When I reached her house, her car was still in the driveway, so my hopes were high that she was still home. I parked on the street outside her house and jogged up her driveway to knock on the door. Surprise, surprise, there was no answer, yet again. I scowled as I knocked a second time but much harder. How many times was she planning to freeze me out? My knuckles stung from the banging, but I didn't care. If it got her attention, then all of the pain would be worth it. However, there was still no response after five minutes of me banging on the door. Not over the phone or from the front door. As a backup option, I circled around to the backyard to see if I would find any better luck with the back patio door. I felt like a Peeping Tom, but desperate times called for desperate measures. I tried the back patio door, hoping that if she really was inside that the sound of my fist against the glass would grab her attention.

"Where is she!" I shouted in frustration. My nerves were now up in my throat, putting me in a chokehold. The stress was killing me, and at this point, I wanted to start ripping my hair out.

My last resort was to check the window on the other side of the house that had a view of her kitchen. The bottom of the window was just above my eye-level so it took all of my strength and balance to tippy-toe as high as I could to look inside. All of those years of yoga were finally paying off. I held onto the window ledge as I tried to hoist myself up, but because I was wearing sandals, my feet lost grip against the wall and I nearly slipped and fell to the ground. Luckily, I caught myself on the wooden fence behind me that separated the neighbor's backyard from Sidney's just in time to keep me standing and uninjured. Being more careful this time, I took a second look through the window. Now I could finally see the top of Sidney's head standing in the middle of the kitchen by the sink. As I put my feet flat on the ground again to catch my breath, a huge sigh of relief washed over me, knowing, at the very least, that my best friend was safe at home. Although the ominous feeling in my stomach still hadn't gone away, I tried to focus on the positives and convince myself that she must have been too busy cooking to hear her phone or didn't want to check it with dirty hands.

I took a big inhale as I braced myself to anchor my arms onto the window ledge to get a better look. My feet dangled against the wall as my arms and shoulders did the heavy lifting. However, when I looked inside her kitchen once again, there was nothing in the world that was going to be enough to prepare me for what I saw. Once I spotted Sidney, my eyes trailed down to the biggest butcher knife I'd ever seen clutched in her hands like she was the killer in some 1980s horror movie. Her hands trembled as she gripped the butcher knife, raised it in the air above her head, and slammed it down on a wooden cutting board on the counter. The knife collided with a booming crash, followed by Sidney's desperate cry at the top of her lungs. Although I couldn't see her face, her cry didn't sound like sadness or depression. I continued to observe her as I watched her wiggle the knife out of the cutting board and raise it in the air again. She slammed it down again but this time it was clear she was going through rage and a desire for destruction. Sidney turned her body closer to the sink, which gave me a better view of her profile. From the side, her eyes were wild with an empty flame as she gazed off into the distance with the knife standing upright, stabbed through the middle of the cutting board. As much as I hated to say it, my best friend looked positively possessed.

"Sidney, Sidney!" I cried out as I banged my hand against her window.

Somehow, there was still no response from her, even though we were no more than eight feet away from each other. Determined to get her attention, I continued hitting her window, trying to find the thin line between being loud enough for her to notice me without breaking through the glass and cutting my hand. No matter how many times I bashed my palm against her window, Sidney didn't hear any of it.

Was she wearing headphones or something that I couldn't see?

How could she still not hear me when I was so close to her! I groaned with impatience as my anxiety started to take over. My heart was racing so fast it was like I was in the middle of running a marathon. Sidney must have been so distracted that she was completely in her own world. Scowling in frustration, I dropped down from her window and went back to the back patio door to see if there was anything in her backyard that could help me. If she was going to ignore every sign I gave her, then she left me with no choice but to break in. Who knew what she was capable of with that giant butcher knife? Whatever it was, I wasn't stalling any longer to find out.

Scanning the backyard, I saw a glass table and metal patio furniture, but unless I became the hulk and didn't care about the destruction around me enough to throw a table and chairs through a glass patio door, I needed to find a better option. Sidney was looking the crazy type of scary, but I wasn't that desperate just yet. As I turned to look around one more time, my eyes narrowed in on a rake leaning against the wall—bingo! I rushed toward the wooden rake and ran back to the door like a battering ram as I used the force of my weight to bust an opening big enough to get me into her house. The wooden handle nearly split in half as I tried to ram it into the glass next to the handle. After a few tries, my palms were raw from the friction on the wood so I had to find another option. Damn, that's either some thick strong glass or a cheap rake, I thought to myself.

"Think, Ava, think!" I cried out with my hands up in the air. With each passing second, I was losing more time to save my best friend from potentially seriously hurting herself or her husband, if he was in there with her. I gasped and thought, oh my gosh, has she snapped on Alex?

I tried to figure out another solution, but my head was just filled with the image of Sidney in her kitchen twirling around the biggest knife in the world like it was nothing. Even though she used sarcasm to cope instead of dealing with her emotions way too much, she was never someone I would have pinned as emotionally unstable to the point of violence. But seeing her in her kitchen, I stood corrected. The only thing I needed to do was to get to her as fast as I could.

"Is there anything else here?" I asked myself aloud.

Like a gift from God, I noticed a brick at the edge of her patio by a pile of untouched gardening tools and a bag of fertilizer. A brick was exactly what I needed. I ran as fast as I could to grab it and without any hesitation, threw it at the back patio door. The brick smashed through the glass with a high-pitched crash, slid through her kitchen floor, and scattered shards of glass on the ground. I carefully stuck my hand through the hole to unlock the back door. Finally, after what felt like forever, the door opened, and I stepped inside Sidney's home. I don't know what it was that had Sidney in an emotional chokehold, but even me breaking into her home still wasn't enough to overcome the trance she was in. She was simply standing by the kitchen sink with the butcher knife back in her hands. For the first time all morning, the possible repercussions of my actions were finally starting to get to me. I loved my best friend, but I truly had no idea what she was going to do at that moment. Whatever happened, I needed to approach with the utmost caution if I wanted both of us to get out of this situation without any harm.

"Sidney, Sidney, Sidney baby, what's wrong?" I asked in a cautious, soft voice as I slowly stepped closer to her.

With my arms spread out like I was in an Indiana Jones movie, I carefully avoided any glass while I inched closer to her. She let out a heavy exhale, which let me know that she was aware of my presence to some extent, but she refused to look up or say anything to me. I suppose in a moment as stressful as this, I couldn't complain about whatever win I could get.

"How about we put down the knife?" I suggested sweetly, but there was still no response or further acknowledgement from Sidney. Her eyes were laser-focused on the center of the cutting board, which I could only imagine was an imaginary target of a certain someone's face.

After the slowest two minutes of my life, I carefully made my way to Sidney's side and kept a safe distance between me and any range of motion she could have if she swung the knife. I kept my back close to the refrigerator and stove. If I wanted to end this quickly, I had to think fast and get that knife out of her hands. From the corner of my eye, I saw a frying pan hanging against the counter by the stove. This was going to be my one shot out of this safely. All in one quick and swift motion, I grabbed the frying pan from the hanging rack and swung it over Sidney's hands like a baseball player hitting a homerun. The knife flew out of her hands and tumbled into the sink with a loud clatter, which gave me just enough time to drop the pan and wrap my arms around Sidney to trap her. I was sure a hug was something she was in desperate need of right now, but I also needed to make sure her arms were secured so that she didn't have any chance of reaching the knife again. However, as I caged Sidney in my arms, her legs gave out and her full body weight was held up only by the strength of my arms and back.

We fell to the ground together as I failed to keep her held up. She tumbled over out of my arms and lay limp on the ground on her side with her shoulders shaking as a mournful wailing started to erupt from her throat. I quickly slid on the kitchen floor closer to her to pull her upright and rest her head on my shoulder. Sidney sobbed deeply in my neck with her salty tears running down my chest. There was no strength left in her body, just an endless stream of tears that were going down her face like her life depended on it. It was almost scary seeing her like this. I could see my best friend, but she felt like a shell of the person she used to be. Sidney and I remained on her floor for almost twenty minutes before she let out the biggest shriek. Snot was running down her nose and she was gasping for breath in between each cry.

"HE HAS ANOTHER CHILD!" she screamed like bloody murder. Her voice broke down again by the end of the sentence like her emotions were just hit by a semi-truck.

My eyes widened in absolute shock. Things had already been bad enough when she'd suspected her husband was cheating on her, but to not only confirm its truth but also to find out there was another baby involved was beyond me. My jaw fell right open, unable to keep my surprise disguised as I tried to be a support system for my best friend. But no matter what I could do for Sidney, this whole situation was bigger than the two of us now. Even though Sidney wasn't ready to tell everyone else about what was going on, I needed backup, and I needed it now. In life, shit gets rough, but that's why you have best friends who will always have your back. I dialed Leeta first knowing she had the furthest drive before calling Nina and Hannah to drop whatever they were doing to come immediately. We were having a code red, and it was not a drill.

Within forty minutes, all of the ladies arrived and flooded Sidney's driveway like an FBI raid. Because I couldn't bear to leave her alone, I instructed everyone to enter through the back patio door the way I did. Each person took big steps as they crossed the shattered glass to find Sidney and me still sitting on the ground huddled together. Without a word, Nina and Leeta each grabbed Sidney's arms to lift her up and move her to the living room so that we could all sit together on the couch and find out what exactly had happened. Hannah stayed back to grab a broom to sweep up most of the glass to avoid anyone getting hurt. I started to brew up some hot chamomile tea to help settle everyone's adrenaline while hiding the butcher knife under all of the cleaning supplies below the sink.

After a few minutes of settling in, Hannah and I entered the living room with five cups of tea in our hands. Sidney was swaddled in an afghan on the couch like she was rescued from a near drowning experience, with Nina and Leeta squished on each side of her tightly. Nina rubbed her leg while Leeta hugged her around her shoulders. Everyone came running at the notice that Sidney was handling a knife like a psycho, but no one knew the big secret that I knew.

As I took a seat on the armchair, Sidney finally looked up at me and gave me the saddest eyes I'd ever seen. They were puffy and bloodshot like an old Freddy Cougar victim. I took a deep breath to prepare myself, knowing that I was going to have to be the one to break the news to everyone else.

"Alex has been cheating on her," I announced on Sidney's behalf. The room stood still for a moment, and it was as if we were all paused like in a movie. No one dared to move or make a sound, as if staying still was going to make this reality any less real. "And his side-chick has a baby."

Leeta innocently gasped as Nina balled the hand on Sidney's lap into a fist and Hannah shook her head, looking off into the distance blankly. Even though it wasn't my life or my news to share, it still felt awful to say out loud. It only made me wonder more how much pain Sidney was going through, knowing her marriage was falling apart. As expected, Sidney was still in no condition to talk about what happened herself.

"How did she find out?" Hannah questioned in a low voice.

"What is she gonna do?" Leeta commented with tears beginning to well in her eyes as she brushed Sidney's hair out of her eyes.

"Gosh, I can't imagine going through something like that," Nina remarked, somehow still comparing her life to everyone else's even though she was acting as if she didn't have her own shit that she was secretly dealing with too.

"That's all I know. She told me yesterday, but when I called to check up on her, she wasn't picking up my calls so I came over and found her like this," I pointed to Sidney.

Everyone turned to Sidney, who seemed like she was starting to calm down from the adrenaline and shock of the news. Her eyes weren't as glossy and empty, and she was no longer shaking. Nina and Leeta both snuggled closer to her for comfort while Hannah and I sat by them in silent comradery. Sidney was never someone we had to worry about, so figuring out how to help was new for all of us.

"If and when you're ready to talk, we're all here to listen, okay?" Leeta told Sidney sweetly as she gave her a warm squeeze.

Sidney showed no signs of being ready to talk. Her lips were pressed firmly in a line, shut tighter than a bank vault. She lowered her eyes to the ground and simply breathed through the pain. I shook my head to signal to everyone else to give her time and space. Whether or not she wanted to talk about what happened in front of everyone was up to Sidney. Of course, we all knew it would be better to speak up instead of harboring everything inside, but we couldn't force her to do anything she didn't want to do. We all sat around the living room quietly for almost an hour when Sidney lifted her head off of Leeta's shoulder. Everyone sat up straight, perked up with energy and attention to our best friend.

"I've had a bad feeling for a few months now," she started off with a slow and heavy breath. "So this morning I checked his computer. It had a new password, but I figured it out anyway. Maybe I was wrong for breaking into his computer, but I was right for wanting to do so. When a woman has a strong intuition about something, you know it's probably right."

"What did you find out?" Hannah asked as she leaned closer with her cup of tea in hand.

After a long pause, Sidney finally replied, "Emails with photos of some baby I'd never seen in my life." She shook her head as she looked at the ground.

"Oh... well, maybe, on the bright side, he's a godfather or something and he was waiting to tell you the news," Leeta chimed in optimistically. Nina shot her a look to shut up because reckless optimism wasn't the best solution to every problem like Leeta thought.

"There were also his pay stubs with deductions for child support," Sidney replied flatly, squashing all of Leeta's hope.

"I'm gonna kill him," Nina muttered under her breath as she

gritted her teeth.

"Does he know you know?" Hannah wondered.

"Yeah, I confronted him this morning. And do you know what he had the audacity to say?" Sidney's voice was getting stronger with rage now that she was slowly moving on from sadness. "He said I was in the wrong for breaking into his computer and not him for having an affair and knocking up some hussy on the side. It's like he forgot we are literally married. I had to remind him we were bound by vows and promises to be faithful and love one another and that didn't include being a cheater!"

"What did he say to that?" I asked.

"He had nothing to say so he stormed out and left for work. Who knows if he's even coming back tonight or if he's just gonna stay with his sneaky-link." Sidney gagged at the word "sneaky link," rightfully sick to her stomach at her husband's infidelity.

All the ladies sat around the living room with a blank stare as we let all of the information settle in our minds. Another fifteen minutes of silence went by as we tried to process Sidney's situation. It wasn't like the rest of us hadn't experienced a liar and a cheater in our lives before, but none of us were married when it happened. Getting cheated on while dating didn't necessarily mean it hurt less, but the repercussions of infidelity in marriage were far bigger. Leaving an awful man you were dating was easier. You could simply stop talking to him one day and decide to never see him again. But getting divorced was a whole new ballgame that was going to take months of dealing with the trauma over and over while fighting over assets and money.

Out of nowhere, breaking the silence, Hannah said, "Children are a blessing. Maybe there's a silver lining. Blended families have become more popular over the last few years. Sometimes people just have to do what's best for the child, who didn't ask to come here." I could tell that a part of her was no longer talking about Sidney's situation and was thinking about her own daughter. "Sid, I know you're hurting, but this could turn out to be something beautiful, a true blessing." We all tilted our heads back and turned to look at Hannah with glaring, confused eyes.

Sidney leaned forward to look at her and replied, "Hannah, you know I love you, but that's that White people shit right there!" We all burst out laughing, including Hannah. Although Hannah's comment was poorly timed, I was secretly grateful for the comic relief it gave to everyone, especially Sidney. Since coming to her home, this was the first time I saw the old Sidney again.

"No, no, no, that's not just White people stuff. Black people do blended families too," Hannah tried to explain but there was no way in hell she was convincing anyone with that nonsense. We were way too early and sober into this mess to be thinking Sidney's husband's side-chick and baby were a blessing in disguise. Leeta carefully pulled her arm out from behind Sidney's neck and grabbed the couch pillow behind her to slap Hannah across the head with it.

"Shut the fuck up! Bad timing, Hannah, bad timing," Leeta scolded. Even though Leeta was a Care Bear, she also had her mama bear moments too. We all just shook our heads and laughed hysterically through the pain. Sometimes you gotta laugh to keep from crying. I looked around at my best friends and wished we could stay in this moment, laughing forever, so we didn't have to come back to face reality.

After the laughter died down, Hannah made yet another poorly timed comment when she said, "While we're on the subject, Nina, what's been going on with your situation? We can all tell that something is wrong. You're not happy. Now is the time for you to spill it!" Knowing Hannah for as long as I have, I knew that this was her way to help get the limelight off Sidney, but it meant throwing Nina under the bus in the process.

Taken back by shock, Nina snapped, "How is my life 'on the subject'?" Nina paused and took a deep breath. We could see her eyes watering.

"Don't start. I have no more tears left to cry," I warned both Nina and Hannah.

The room went quiet again. I could see that Nina was going through the works in her head now that Hannah had opened Pandora's Box. With great hesitation, Nina took a sip of tea before preparing herself to speak.

"Well, since y'all are all in my business, thinking you know, but you don't…" Her voice trailed off as she gathered herself to speak.

"I'm not all in your business thinking anything, that's Hannah," I said as I placed my hand across my chest with a playful look of confusion to lighten up the mood.

Nina gave a weak smile as she acknowledged my efforts before softly saying, "The one thing my husband wants so desperately, that I can't give him, are children. He wants lots of screaming children running around laughing, playing. He wants a huge family, but I've not been able to conceive. I feel like an outcast. I feel like a failure. My biological clock is at the 13th hour, and I'm always so afraid that one day he's going to wake up and leave me for a younger woman who can give him the family he deserves," Nina confessed in one quick breath, like ripping off a Band-Aid, before taking a long, deep sigh.

Our mouths flew open. We were in shock! We all just thought Nina didn't want to have children. None of us could believe she kept this bottled inside all these years. Strangely, I didn't know whether to be sad, empathetic, or pissed!

Secrets

Nina stared down at her hands fidgeting in her lap in silence. Her sudden surge of confidence just a minute earlier had disappeared now that the words escaped her lips and her dark secret was finally out. We sat around the living room waiting for someone to make the first move. Although I knew this was not her intention, I still gave Hannah some side-eye for causing more trouble. Leave it to Hannah to make a bad situation worse. It was bad enough having one woman in distress, but now we had two. Great.

Ironically, now Sidney was the one rubbing Nina's thigh in comfort instead of the other way around. The two women gave each other hugs as they sniffled and reached for a tissue at the same time. They exchanged eyes when they realized their telepathy and let out a small giggle each. Their laughter was like medicine in the room filled with uncertainty and worry. The rest of us joined in with a small laugh, giving us each some space to breathe.

"You don't have to talk about anything you don't want to," I finally said, breaking the silence.

"No, I—" Nina started and stopped to take another deep inhale. "I think I need to finally talk about this. I mean, I didn't expect to today, let alone in the middle of Sidney having an emotional breakdown, but I guess you can't always choose opportunities. Sometimes they just choose you." Nina shrugged her shoulders and let out a small, forced laugh.

"Or you have a best friend to choose for you," Hannah joked lightly. Leeta, Sidney, and I all shot Hannah a look in unison. She shrugged her shoulders and held her hands up in surrender. "It was just a joke." Sometimes I wondered if she liked to push buttons on purpose or if she really didn't know the mistakes she made. Even after knowing her for most of my life, I still had trouble making out the difference when it came to Hannah.

"Lots of women have trouble getting pregnant. It's not just you, so please don't be so hard on yourself," Leeta said to redirect the topic back to Nina appropriately. She squeezed Nina's hand tightly and whispered a few words to herself, most likely doing some healing technique to send her good vibes.

"I know that, but I still can't help it," Nina exhaled with her head hung low. It was truly heartbreaking to see her so down on herself when we all knew her as an incredibly confident and, at times, arrogant woman.

"Have you tried alternative options?" Sidney asked.

"We've been trying in vitro for a few years now, and I can't even tell you how many times it has failed at this point. It's at least ten thousand dollars per round! So much of our savings has been drained because my stupid body just won't cooperate," Nina confessed as she slapped her stomach in frustration and more tears began to fall down her cheeks.

"Don't say that! You and your body are not stupid. IVF doesn't work for everyone, and there's nothing wrong with that," Leeta interrupted as she grabbed Nina's hand from hitting herself again.

"Again, I know that, but I still can't help it! None of this is according to any plan I ever imagined for my life. I thought I was going to get married first amongst the five of us, have a beautiful family by my mid-thirties, and be the best mom who took her kids to soccer practice every day and had freshly baked cookies ready when they got home. You know, the stuff you see in catalogs or TV shows. But I haven't accomplished any of those goals! Under my own standards, I'm the biggest failure," Nina broke out into a sob as she threw her hands in the air in defeat. She cried like a sprinkler on the first day of a hot summer morning. The tears flowed endlessly down her cheeks and dripped down, making puddles on her lap.

"Nina, I love you, but you are crazy. Your standards are crazy. Do you have any idea how idealistic all of those goals are? None of us have met your goals, so if you're a failure, so are we," I reasoned with her as I leaned forward to get her attention in the middle of her crying fit.

"Half of us are still single, if that makes you feel better," Hannah commented. I had to admit that that remark stung a little, but she was right.

"I don't know why I'm like this. I truly understand what you guys are saying, and maybe I can get a little intense sometimes about how I think things should play out—" Nina started to say when Sidney interjected.

"A little intense?"

"Okay, really intense, alright? But that's just what I've always imagined ever since I was a kid. My dream has always been to be a mom. I spent all of my pretend time playing with baby dolls and taking care of them the way my mom took care of me. It just really feels like a knife to my heart when I think about how I'll never be that." Nina's voice broke by the end of her sentence, devastated by the thought of never becoming a mother. For as long as I'd known Nina, she'd never talked about how much she wanted kids and to be a mother, so none of us knew that this was such a big deal to her. She'd mentioned from time to time that she wanted to have kids someday, but it seemed more like something that she was excited for instead of something she dreamed about.

"Who said you're out of time? You can still be a mom," Leeta argued back as she scooted closer.

"I'm in my forties. Do you know how hard it is to get pregnant this late? I kept telling myself throughout my thirties that I still had time, but after I turned forty, I've spent so many nights depressed and crying about how I wasted so much of my youth not having gone to the doctor sooner or trying other methods to start a family sooner. I feel so much less of a woman not being able to do the one thing that my body is supposed to be able to do. Not to mention how much Michael wants a family. Do you know what it's like to look your husband in the eyes and tell him the pregnancy test was negative yet again?" Nina tilted her head back as she tried to blink away the tears welling up in her eyes. After she composed herself, she continued, "He's been so kind about it, but I'm sure it's going to start to frustrate him. It's sure as hell been frustrating me! I just want to give him the one thing he so desperately wants, but for whatever reason I just can't. My body just won't. I'm the biggest failure of a wife. I keep talking about living the most perfect life, but it's all just been the biggest lie."

More tears streamed down her face like a waterfall as she dropped her head into her hands. Sidney rubbed her back as Leeta leaned over to rub her arm. I got up from beside Hannah to occupy the seat on Nina's other side and rested my head on her shoulder. Although there was nothing any of us could say to make her feel better, the least we could do was make sure she knew she wasn't alone through all of this.

"Oh, Nina, you're doing just fine. You are not a failure! No one's life is perfect," I told her as I slipped my arms around her waist to give her a hug.

Leeta reached to grab another tissue for Nina from the coffee table, but the box was empty. Nina immediately noticed and picked up her purse to dig for a travel-sized packet of tissues instead. She pushed her phone aside as she reached into the bottom of her giant purse. She pulled one tissue out to wipe her tears and dab her nose. From the corner of my eye, I saw a light flash inside of her purse as she set it back down on the ground tucked behind her feet.

"Have you talked to Michael about any of this?"

"Honestly, I'm too scared to. I was terrified enough just telling you guys. He's been so sweet about each failure, but I'm scared that he's going to reach his limit and try to find someone else who can give him what he wants. The older I get, the more I feel like that woman isn't going to be me. I'm just a failure," she cried out and covered her face with a new tissue.

"That's crazy! Just because you might not be able to bear children doesn't mean that you're not the love of his life! And if he's willing to throw you away just because of one thing that you can't control, then he doesn't deserve someone as amazing as you!" Sidney raised her voice with a fiery passion I hadn't heard from her in a while. Part of me wondered if she was telling Nina, herself, or both.

"I agree! I don't think it's good for you to beat yourself up over something you genuinely can't control. It's not like you don't want kids or anything. It's not your fault, and so you don't blame yourself like it is," Hannah explained softly.

"Do you really think so? I just feel like all of the pressure lies on my shoulders and I just can't seem to deliver, no matter how badly I want to," Nina replied weakly.

"YES!" The room erupted in unison.

"This is not your fault in the slightest!"

As we consoled Nina, I noticed the tension in Sidney's shoulders was finally starting to loosen up. Like anyone in distress, she just needed some time to burn through her energy and breathe through the pain. Even though it wasn't ideal to switch from one woman's pain to another, it was still relieving to see that Sidney was starting to make progress with her situation. Just because we were focusing on Nina right now didn't mean that I had easily forgotten the start of the domino in the first place. The image of Sidney swinging around a giant butcher knife still haunted my thoughts like the boogieman in a child's nightmare.

As Nina leaned forward to blow her nose, I tapped Sidney on the shoulder and whispered quietly, "Are you okay?"

Sidney looked at me with a small smile and nodded her head. I squeezed her shoulder and smiled back, knowing that she was in a much better place than she was earlier. I knew that Sidney was going to be okay, no matter what the outcome of Alex's infidelity was, but what mattered most was that Sidney knew it too.

"Hey, Sidney, do you want us to stay here when your husband comes back?" Hannah questioned. Although it seemed a bit early to ask, it was still a question in the back of everyone's mind.

"Sure, I think that might be nice. Thanks, everyone," Sidney smiled at each of us.

In order to give Nina some time to breathe out of the spotlight, the rest of us continued with light, casual conversation to pass time until either Sidney or Nina were ready to talk about anything else. As Hannah was talking about something her daughter learned in school, there was a ferocious knock on the door. We all stopped and stared at each other with wide eyes filled with worry about what was coming next. It was getting late in the day, but it still seemed too early for Sidney's husband to be back home already. All five of us braced ourselves as Sidney took a deep breath and picked herself up from the couch to answer the door.

"Are you sure you're ready? I can answer the door," I offered as I stood up from the couch.

"Thanks, Ava. But I have to do this," Sidney said as she put her hand out to stop me.

Each of us held our breath as she left the room. No matter what happened, we were going to stand our ground and protect our best friend in whatever way she needed. The door opened and at first, the only thing we could hear was heavy breathing and then a familiar voice appeared that shocked us all.

"Where's Nina?"

Nina's head snapped up at the sound of Michael's worried voice as he burst through the door and rushed into the living room. His eyes were filled with tears as he ran to Nina's side, grabbed her hands, and pulled her up to her feet. In one swift motion, Michael guided Nina close to him and wrapped his arms around her waist for a hug as he squeezed his eyes tight, shedding the tears in his eyes like the first drops of rainfall in the winter. In that moment, it felt like watching a movie, seeing how Michael and Nina looked at each other like they were the only ones in the room together. Leeta and I both stood up from the couch to give them some space. She took a seat beside Hannah and I remained standing by the entrance, where Sidney joined me.

"You're not a failure, Nina. Not in the least bit. I love you so much and I never want you to doubt that a day in your life," Michael told her as he tried to fight back more tears.

"What are you talking about?"

"You must have called me by accident, but I heard you talking about our pregnancy journey and say you were at Sidney's house. I tried to call you almost a dozen times but you didn't pick up any of my calls or answer my text messages, so I left work early to come here and tell you myself that you have never been a failure in my eyes. I don't care about how many times IVF didn't work for us. You are the love of my life, and we will figure out whatever comes next for us together. This is not all on you," he said before giving her a kiss on her forehead.

"Michael, I—I don't know what to say…" Nina blushed.

"Truthfully, I wish you'd told me sooner, but I understand how hard it must have been for you. However, we are in this together, so we both have to work through the ups and downs. That's what marriage means. I'm sorry that I didn't notice how badly this was affecting you. I wish there was something I could have done sooner to help you through all of your pain." Michael hugged her again even more tightly this time.

"I just didn't know how to say any of this to anyone. It was scary worrying if another round was going to fail again, and, honestly, I was really embarrassed. So many women have kids every day. Look at how many women get pregnant and don't even want their baby? How come I can't make one no matter how badly I want to? I didn't know how to deal with those feelings, so I just bottled everything up and pretended it was okay," Nina explained as she hung her head in shame.

"It's really okay. At the end of the day, if IVF doesn't work, it doesn't work. There are still other options we haven't explored yet. We can go through a surrogacy or even adoption. It doesn't matter what method we use, Nina. You and I are going to be amazing parents to whatever child comes our way. Whether or not our child is one you physically birth, that child will still be our child and we will be the perfect family you always dreamed about," he smiled warmly.

A small part of me was worried that all of us standing around watching such a private conversation unfold in front of us was an invasion of privacy, but it was just simply too beautiful to look away from. It was undeniable how much Michael had always loved Nina, but to know that he was not fazed one bit about the hurdles they had been going through in their pregnancy journey was truly inspiring. Michael was the kind of man who set the bar for how all men needed to treat women. He was understanding, patient, willing to learn and listen, and worked hard at making a relationship work. Watching Michael and Nina's relationship so emotionally raw made me feel really good about my romantic position in life. Sure, being forty and single wasn't ideal, but there were so many times I could have settled for someone who was less than what I deserved. Watching Michael reminded me that I was worthy of spending the rest of my life with someone who would do anything to make our relationship work, regardless of how hard it got. No man that I dated before had ever given me that feeling, which must have been why none of them ever worked out—thank goodness for that too!

Michael, being the new standard for men in my eyes, settled and, funnily enough, brought tears to my eyes. My vision started to blur knowing that my best friend had one of the best men I knew taking care of her, especially as they went through such a difficult and emotionally draining journey. I sniffled quietly and tried to hide my tears when I heard a louder sniffle behind my shoulder. I turned around to see Sidney with red eyes as she wiped her cheeks with the back of her hand. Across the room, Leeta and Hannah were both huddled together with tissues covering their faces as well. Somehow, we'd all fallen to tears watching Nina and Michael. Michael took a step back to look at his wife with a beaming smile and rubbed the side of her arms. Nina nodded her head and tried to hide her face with her hands as she searched for her packet of tissues somewhere on the couch. I stepped forward toward Michael as he dropped his hands to his side and reached out for a hug.

"Thank you for being the best husband to my best friend. I'm so happy that you are in our lives and taking great care of Nina," I said as I patted his back in a quick hug.

In the middle of such a tender and sweet moment, a low rumbling sounded off nearby. We all turned to Sidney, who stood with her arms folded as she leaned against the wall. I couldn't tell if she was still too distracted with Nina and Michael or if she was ignoring the garage opening because it meant that her cheating husband had just gotten home. Sidney smiled as she watched over our best friend, and I could tell she was genuinely happy for Nina, despite her own marriage hanging on by a thread.

I could hear Alex's footsteps growing louder as he quickly approached the living room. All five women stood their ground with cold expressions on our faces as we waited for him to arrive. I waited by Sidney's side and stood firmly as a protective wall between her and her husband. Within a minute, Alex entered the room with an irritable look on his face. His forehead was creased and his frown was so deep I could still see it through the gigantic bush on his face he called a beard. I looked him up and down with disgust before rolling my eyes and turning my back to him. Alex watched Sidney with a clenched jaw as Sidney kept her eyes on Nina and Michael instead.

"Look at me, Sidney. We need to talk," Alex's deep voice bellowed.

"About what? About the woman you cheated on me with? Or the child you've known about and been paying child support for? You tell me, Alex," Sidney snapped back without breaking her stare.

"What about you breaking into my computer? Reading my private emails? I'm not saying I didn't mess up, but you can't act like you didn't do your share of mistakes either," he argued back like the dumb man he was. Who was he kidding with an argument like that? Heat boiled up to my neck listening to Alex desperately try to defend himself. Within seconds, it was too much for me to listen to without chiming in myself.

"You must be out of your mind if you think cheating on your wife and keeping your side-chick's baby is remotely comparable to rightfully going through a lying and cheating man's computer. You can't say shit about what she did, since she was right to do it. Were you ever going to tell her?" I shouted back at him as I took a step closer to him. There was not a bone in my body afraid of what he could do to me, there was only fire running through my veins.

"Ava, I know you mean well, but I think this might be better handled between Sidney and Alex themselves," Michael said gently as he walked up to keep Alex and me apart. I shook my head as I looked at his lying face and felt a relapse of heat from Lying-Ass Larry. There was a chance I was taking this a little more personally than I needed to, but regardless, Sidney was my best friend, and I wasn't going to roll over and let her get treated poorly by a man who clearly didn't deserve her.

"You're lucky you even have a chance with Sidney. Do you know how good she is and how shit you are?" I spat back at him.

"It's okay, Ava. I got this. I know I originally wanted you guys here, but after thinking things through, I think Michael is right and Alex and I should talk about this in private," Sidney announced softly behind me.

We all waited a minute in case Sidney changed her mind, but she remained firm about her decision, so we had no other option but to respect it. Leeta, Nina, Hannah, and I made eyes at each other and agreed to pack up our things and head out. I gave Sidney a hug and Alex another glare before returning to the couch to grab my purse beside Hannah. Each of us grabbed our belongings and tidied up the couch before walking out. I could see Sidney finally looked Alex in the eye but they both remained silent with their arms crossed at each other.

"What ever happened to Larry from Texas?" Hannah chimed in and broke my attention from Sidney. Instantly, I rolled my eyes and let out a heavy sigh.

"Lying-Ass Larry? As usual, Hannah, your timing is the worst," I chuckled, too dumbfounded by her poor timing to not break out in laughter.

We all burst out in laughter at Hannah as she looked back at us with a devilish smile. I knew that Hannah was doing this on purpose to once again lighten the mood, but did she have to bring Larry into this? I shook my head at her and playfully waved my finger in front of her like a parent punishing a child.

"I guess it's your turn next, Ava!" Leeta cried out playfully.

"That story would take the whole night with a round of drinks at the bar," I remarked as I shook my head with wide eyes. Lying-Ass Larry was a journey, to say the least.

"You ain't lyin'!" Leeta chimed in.

"Why don't we go to the bar then?" Hannah suggested out of the blue.

I spun around to look at Hannah as I clutched my purse. She beamed back at me before pulling out her phone to check the time. She showed us her screen, which read five pm. The four of us exchanged looks as we contemplated going to the bar together. The last time we'd hung out altogether had been my birthday dinner, but we rarely got to hang out with each other for this long anymore, and certainly not this early.

"That's true, if we leave now, we can make it for happy hour," Leeta nodded excitedly. She was already bouncing at the thought of a girl's happy hour.

I subtly shook my head as I signaled to Leeta and Hannah about Sidney and Nina. As much as I would have loved to have a girls' happy hour after the day I had, I didn't want to impose on them handling their private marital issues. However, the longer Hannah and Leeta looked at me with longing eyes like children waiting for candy after going to the doctor's office, I started to come around to the idea.

Before I could make a decision, Nina cut in and said, "You know, with the day we've all had, I think we need to head to the bar."

We all snapped our heads to Nina standing behind us. She had the biggest smile on her face now that her secret was out and some of the weight on her shoulders had been lifted. As her best friend, it instantly put me in such a good mood seeing her so happy again.

"Are you sure? I know some of us have other things to deal with." I tried to reason, giving her a way out in case she felt obligated to join.

"I'm okay, don't worry, Ava," Nina replied with a gentle smile before turning to her husband and lowering her voice to say, "Do you mind if I go with the girls for a bit? We can finish our conversation when I get back home."

"Yeah, of course. Go decompress, and I'll be waiting for you at home when you feel ready to talk about everything you've been going through. I love you, Nina." Michael gave her another kiss on the forehead and then one on the lips before resting his forehead on hers.

"I love you too, Michael. You truly are the perfect husband."

Nina and Michael embraced each other in another hug as Leeta, Hannah, and I all watched the tender moment. It took everything in me not to accidentally say "aw" at the sight of them being so sweet to each other. Michael waved to all of us and patted Alex on the shoulder on his way out. They exchanged a silent look only men could understand before Michael disappeared around the corner and out the front door. The rest of us took this as our cue to also head out as well.

"I'll walk you guys out," Sidney suggested as she pointed to the door.

"It's okay," I said, but she shook her head.

"No, I want to."

The four of us stood side by side next to the front door to each give Sidney one last hug before we left. Honestly, I couldn't remember the last time we hugged each other this much within a few hours but it just felt suiting with all of the events that unfolded in this house today. I was the last one in line to hug Sidney and took my sweet time doing so. Being the only person she'd willingly confided in, I gave her an extra-long squeeze and rocked side to side as I held her in my arms. Sidney was one of the last people who deserved to be cheated on like this by her husband, so it was still somewhat of a shock that was really happening to her.

"Thank you so much for everything, Ava," Sidney whispered in my ear before stepping back. "Thank you all. I wanted to tell you guys eventually what was going on, but before this morning, it was all just a hunch. Believe me, if I was wrong, I would have much rather told that story than me being right."

"Ain't that the truth," Leeta scoffed. We all waited in the doorway, each of us reluctant to actually leave now that it was time to finally go.

"But I know I'm going to be okay. Regardless of what happens, Alex and I will figure it out, so I don't want you guys to worry about me, okay? When have I ever not been able to take care of myself?" Sidney chuckled softly before stopping suddenly. "Minus this morning."

"Well, in our defense, you were literally bat-shit crazy this morning," I mentioned not so casually.

"Okay, but minus this morning!"

"We trust you. We're just going to go to Big Ben's up the street, so we'll be less than a mile away from you. If you need us, call or text, and we'll be back here faster than you can hang up the phone," Hannah finally said after a long pause.

With her creased forehead and prominent frown, I could tell that she was still incredibly worried about Sidney. Hannah, as annoying and socially inept she was at times, was still someone who loved very deeply even though she didn't always know how to show it in the best ways. It took a long time for the rest of the girls to get used to her, but having known Hannah for much longer, it was something that I surprisingly learned to love about her. She was the kind of girl you wanted to hate but couldn't help but love, and I wouldn't have things any other way.

"And no knives," Nina added.

"Okay, I promise. No knives. I love you guys so much," Sidney said with open arms as we gathered for one last group hug.

"We love you too, Sidney."

The Academy Award for Best Liar

A weight was lifted off of my shoulders now that I wasn't the only one who knew Sidney's secret, and especially knowing that she seemed in a much better place to handle it with her husband. I happily nodded my head in the car as I drove behind my friends, completely forgetting the shitstorm that I was about to retell. I most certainly needed a drink if I was going to get into Lying-ass Larry.

"Siri, call Leeta."

"He—" Leeta started when I interrupted.

"Why does Hannah talk so damn much?" I exclaimed irately.

"You know how Hannah is!" Leeta laughed.

"I'm just not ready to talk about this all over again. This man was such a habitual liar, it's embarrassing. I would like to go on with the rest of my life acting like I never knew him. Damn Hannah and her big ass mouth!" I whined as I pulled into the parking lot.

"It's going to be okay! Let's just get to the bar, have a few drinks, and laugh this shit out," Leeta said, trying to cheer me up, but there was no use when it came to Larry.

The bar had a decent crowd, given work hours had just ended, so we were ready to take full advantage of happy hour. The four of us were seated in a booth in the back, thankfully away from any wandering ears who might hear my humiliating story. My hands fidgeted on my lap as I tried to smile, until Hannah looked me dead in the eyes as she turned to me across the table.

"Now, what happened with Larry?" she asked. I sighed and mentally wanted to bash my head against the table. Although I loved Hannah dearly, there was definitely a reason why I didn't tell her sooner.

"Damn, Hannah. Okay, let's order drinks first before we get into it, because we're definitely gonna need some drinks for this fuckin' story," I groaned.

"Margaritas all around?" Nina asked as she got up from the booth. We nodded as she disappeared to the bar. I grabbed some peanuts from the basket on the table just to give my hands something to do while I tried to relax and figure out where exactly in the story to start.

"Okay, so do you guys remember Nicole?" I finally said after a long pause.

"I don't think so," Hannah replied.

"Y'all remember Nicole, with the six kids whose husband owns that construction company over on Second street," I emphasized more clearly as Nina returned and hopped back into her seat.

"Oh yeah, that Nicole. I cannot imagine taking care of six kids, wow," Hannah said as she shook her head.

"Well, she was the one who introduced me to Larry. At first, he wasn't my type. He flew in to see me the first month we met, but then I had to fly out for business at the last minute. I felt so bad! But he was determined and flew in to see me the next month again and there were instant sparks. He wasn't the quirky nerdy guy I assumed he was just off conversation. He was actually pretty cool! Or so I thought. I thought to myself he's got a little hood in him. I think I like him! We met for brunch and then later that evening we met for dinner. Since he lived in Texas, he flew back out the next day, but surprisingly our conversations became more frequent, and I really started digging him. He would ask me questions about marriage all the time. But they were just general questions—at least that's what it seemed to me. Y'all know me, I never like to assume someone is really digging me like that unless you tell me. If you don't say so, I'm gonna take it as general. You have to be direct with me. We're too grown for the kiddie games!" I said as I threw my hands in the air.

Hannah, Nina, and Leeta all nodded their heads, saying, "Mmhm mmhm."

A server arrived at our table with four frozen strawberry margaritas garnished with fresh strawberries and bits of pineapple on top. Despite being a wine person myself, I couldn't deny how mouthwatering the margaritas looked, especially with how dry my mouth was just thinking about how the hell I was going to get through this story without losing my mind. I took a sip and let the tequila sink in to calm my nerves.

Hannah clapped her hands to get all of our attention and raised her glass with a beaming but devilish smile on her face as she said, "Yes, but now it's time to get to the real meat and potatoes of the story. This sounds like it's about to be juicy!"

Leeta said, "Yeah, and you have no idea just how juicy it's about to get!" Hannah's eyes gleamed as if she was staring at a million dollars. No one loved juicy gossip more than Hannah!

She said, "Hold up, why does Leeta know and I don't?"

I raised my voice and told her, "Do you want to hear the rest of the story or not?"

"Fine! We'll come back to that later," Hannah sang with a smile to butter me up. I rolled my eyes as Leeta and Nina laughed. They knew why I didn't tell Hannah, because, one, she talked too much and two, she got too hyped and wound up to the point of making a bad situation worse. We all loved Hannah, but she was the wild card of the crew. With another deep breath, I shuffled in my seat to get comfortable and dive back into the story of Lying-ass Larry.

After a few weeks of dating, Larry came back into town to see me. Although we hadn't been dating all that long, my stomach was still filled with butterflies at the thought of a good man who changed my mind about him. He was the kind of guy who was confident but not cocky, yet smooth and surprisingly very romantic. Larry wasn't as tall as other men I liked to date, being only five-foot ten, when I needed a man over six feet, but the charm on Larry was more than enough to make up for the missing inches.

Larry booked his stay at a hotel nearby the airport and called me over to have dinner together. Because of the long distance, we hadn't seen each other in almost a month. We had dinner nearby his hotel and had drinks at the hotel bar. It was a nice jazz night, so you know how it goes. A few red wines, some smooth saxophone, and a good-looking man… so we went back to his room and had a good time. Larry wanted me to stay the night with him but I had to get back home so I could prepare for work in the morning. Begrudgingly, I got dressed, gave him a kiss to remember me by, and headed back to my place.

"Did you end up seeing him again?" Hannah piped in with wide eyes.

"Hold on, Hannah. The story is far from over," Leeta shushed.

When I got home, I tried to fall asleep but I was too wired up from everything, so I ended up baking a pie! I had no idea what power this man had over me to bake him a pie, but somehow I did and finally went to bed with only a few hours to spare before waking up for work. Work was a complete blur because all I could think about was seeing Larry one more time before he had to go back, so, after work, I brought the pie to his hotel room where we talked and hung out for a while. Larry and I lay side by side in his bed and cuddled as he rubbed my arm and rested his cheek on the top of my head. I closed my eyes and rested my head on his chest and listened to his heartbeat.

"I have to go back to Texas tomorrow," Larry whispered.

"I know… but do you have to?" I whined.

"I'll only be gone a few days, and then I'll be back to see you again. How about we go on a little trip, just us two somewhere where we can just be together uninterrupted?" He offered with a smile.

"Ooh, you've caught my attention."

"Just show up looking sexy like you do, and I'll handle the rest," Larry chuckled.

"Sounds like a plan to me."

Three weeks later, Larry came back from Texas, and I still had no idea what was happening with our staycation. He rented a car and picked me up from my place without a word, only a smirk on his face as he drove through the city in silence. I stared out the window trying to figure out the plan, but he kept his lips pressed tight until we parked outside of a luxury bed and breakfast hotel in the heart of downtown.

"Welcome to our staycation, Ava."

Larry got out of the car to open my door and ushered me inside the bed and breakfast. There was tranquil classical music playing lightly over the speakers as we rolled our suitcases in, and Larry checked us into a lover's suite on the top floor. Butterflies started to flutter in my stomach again as we ascended in the elevator, standing so close that I could feel his breath on the back of my neck. When we got to the front door, he made me wait as he peeked inside first before letting me go in. There was a trail of rose petals on the ground that led to the bed where there was a charcuterie board, two bottles of wine, and candles lit around the room.

"I can't believe you did all this!" I exclaimed, still in shock.

"Did you bring your sexy self?" he joked with a devilish grin.

"Why yes I did," I winked. We moved the food and drinks from the bed onto the table before jumping straight into sex. After waking up from a well-deserved nap, we had a light lunch, snacking on the food he prepared in the room in bed.

"Tell me more about yourself. What's your family like? What's home back in Texas like?" I questioned as I gazed up at him.

"Well, there's something on my mind that I've been meaning to confess, but I didn't know how to bring it up until now," he said as he shifted in his seat.

"What is it? You can tell me."

"You know I have kids, but I never told you what happened between me and their mother. She passed away, leaving me behind with the kids as a widow. My middle child found her dead on the kitchen floor one afternoon after school and called me and 911 immediately," Larry explained as he looked down.

"Oh my God, that's awful. Is your kid okay? Are you okay?" I gasped.

"Enough time has passed for our wounds to heal, but you never fully recover from a devastation like that, you know?" He looked at me with the saddest brown eyes.

"His ex-wife is dead?!" Hannah shouted.

"Hannah, can you just please listen to the story without interrupting so damn much?" Nina snapped.

"What? You can't hear something like that and not say something," Hannah scoffed as she took another sip. I shook my head as Hannah looked between Leeta and me for backup to support her argument.

"Please continue, Ava," Leeta said, ignoring Hannah.

After hearing about the heartbreaking story of his ex-wife, I made it my goal to make sure I was extra sympathetic and empathetic toward Larry, who was clearly in need of some love and comfort. Every time I thought about how hard it must have been to go through such a traumatizing experience, my heart broke a little more each time. We spent the rest of our weekend cooped in the lover's suite, ordering room service, drinking bottles of wine by our private pool, and had lots and lots of amazing sex. It was truly the perfect staycation, just like Larry had promised. It was going to be another month before we got to see each other again since his high school aged son lived in my area and was about to graduate. We said our goodbyes and waited until Memorial Day weekend to come around for Larry to return.

Waiting for Larry to come back was much harder this time around than before. I felt like we'd gotten closer and finally having a good two and a half days to spend with each other without any external distractions. Larry sent me messages every day to make sure I didn't forget about him as we embarked on our longest time apart from each other.

Memorial Day finally rolled around after what felt like at least six months of waiting instead of just one. He came over to my place straight from the airport, jumped into my arms, bear-hugged me and picked me up with my legs dangling in the air as soon as I opened the door. Throwing all dinner plans out the window, Larry couldn't stay the night as he needed to get to the hotel and prepare for his son's graduation early in the morning. The next day, he sent me a text message that read: "Do you want to continue as though we're just dating or do you prefer to fall in love?"

I stared at the message dumbfounded for a moment as I processed what was going on and my heart instantly started to ignite like a race car engine at the start of a race. A smile danced across my face, tickling my cheeks until they were sore as I reread Larry's message over and over. There was no doubt in my mind when I typed my response: "I prefer to fall in love with you." I sent the message and held the phone to my heart as I squealed in my bedroom like a teenage girl. He responded with "My baby," which only made my heart warm knowing things were going so well between us. However, what I didn't expect was to not hear from Larry for the rest of his visit. I texted him good morning a few times but there was no response. Larry was running around with his three kids and a ton of family members who flew in for the graduation, so I tried to remain understanding and not be a bother. I was sure there were so many things on his plate that a silly good morning text got buried behind all of the bigger responsibilities in his life.

On his last day, I called him so we could catch up and talk after almost the entire holiday weekend of silence. He picked up the call immediately, which was strange, given he had ignored all of my texts throughout the week. I wasn't sure whether or not to bring up my disappointment from his lack of communication, especially when I knew he had family matters going on, but I knew deep down that I deserved to speak up even when it was hard to do so.

"So, I wanted to talk to you about something, but I don't want to come off as insensitive or anything. I just really feel like I have to be honest with you," I started carefully.

"What is it, Ava? You can always be honest with me."

"Why didn't you respond to any of my messages this week?" I asked with hesitation.

"Oh, I was just busy with my family. I'm a father of three grown "kids" and sometimes it gets really chaotic trying to balance all of them and our large family at the same time, especially during times like this," he replied with ease.

"Of course, you're right. I had a feeling it was that, but I just had to ask to make sure." I laughed at myself for being paranoid over nothing.

"Make sure of what?" he replied in a very serious tone that took me by surprise. I paused as I tried to collect my thoughts.

"Just, I don't know. It was unexpected, that's all," I tried to explain.

"Are you saying you don't trust me?" Larry snapped.

"No, of course not!" I exclaimed back, but it was returned with silence. The call was quiet, which then started to make me annoyed as well. How did him not having the decency to text me back become me acting as the villain in this situation? I rolled my eyes and was ready to end the call immediately.

"Let's just talk another time," I replied, to which he agreed, before we both hung up the phone.

"Wow, they sure know how to flip it, don't they?" Hannah roared louder than everyone in the restaurant.

"Not gonna lie, Ava, I do agree with Hannah on this one," Nina shrugged reluctantly as I rubbed my temples and gazed down at my empty cup. The story was only going to get worse, which meant we needed another round of drinks.

"Nina, can we get more drinks?" I said when I finally looked up.

"Is the story that bad?" Hannah questioned with a curious eye.

"Yes," Leeta replied before I could say a word. The table was stunned as we all turned to Leeta who finished the last of her drink. Another round of margaritas arrived at the table after a few minutes. I took a long sip before diving into the next episodic thriller of Lying-ass Larry.

Another week went by of absolute silence between Larry and I, except this time I didn't bother with trying to reach out to him. Sure, I could have been more considerate about him spending time with his family, but I wasn't wrong for bringing up my feelings about it. One day, out of the blue, the doorbell rang at my apartment on a Saturday afternoon. A man with a delivery of a bouquet of flowers and a note stood in my doorway looking for Ava Amore. I signed for the flowers and brought them inside, smelling the roses as I set them down on my kitchen counter. The note read: Thank you for being the amazing woman, leader, romantic creative and Queen. I appreciate you and cherish our connection. -Larry. Just as I finished reading the note, my phone started ringing. It was Larry.

"I'm so sorry, Ava. I shouldn't have reacted like that. I was super busy and exhausted and I took it out on you undeservingly. Is there any way you can forgive me? I believe you just received my flowers. I know it's not enough to say I'm sorry with, but I hope you can accept them. You mean a lot to me and it pains me to know that I've hurt you," he recited all in one breath before I could say hello.

I thought for a long time, leaving silence on the phone until I decided to say, "Fine, I forgive you."

Things between Larry and I got better again and it was nice that we were finally getting back to normal, which made me start to miss him again, especially with my birthday coming up around the corner. It was going to be the first time we celebrated a birthday together, but, unfortunately, Larry had meetings that week and couldn't fly out to see me. He promised to make it up to me, which, given his last surprise, I knew I could trust that he would make it up for me big time.

During the week of my birthday, I woke up to a package at my door, which I could only imagine was a surprise from Larry. However, what I didn't expect was that this would continue every single morning leading up to the day of my birthday. He gave me clear instructions to not open until the day of my birthday, so I made a pile in my living room, even though I was dying to peek. Finally, my birthday came around and my phone chimed, so I ran to see if it was Larry—it was.

He sent me a message saying "Under normal circumstances, I would be making you breakfast in bed right now #goals #birthdaydick" along with a few more R-rated hashtags that made me blush and excited all at the same time. I was in the middle of typing a response to him when his contact flashed on my screen for a call.

"Hey, beautiful, happy birthday," he cried out with enthusiasm.

"Thank you, Larry. I can't believe you got me so many gifts. You really shouldn't have!" I blushed.

"Of course I should have. You are incredible, and I want you to know that. Do you have any plans for tonight?" he asked with a chuckle.

"Yeah, I'm going to dinner with my best girlfriends, but I'll open up your gifts when I get back."

"Perfect. Facetime me when you open your gifts. I want to be there with you as if I was with you in person," he urged.

"You're so silly. Yes, I'll Facetime you," I laughed but secretly found it super sweet.

"I miss you, Ava."

"I miss you too, Larry."

Dinner was an absolute blast at a super fun, Mexican restaurant that served drinks in gigantic cups and gave us all sombreros to wear because Hannah told the server it was my birthday. They gave us some tequila shots on the house, and by the end of dinner, I certainly had to take an Uber back home and leave my car behind overnight. The last thing I wanted on a perfect birthday was a DUI. By the time I got home, I was so sleepy that I simply kicked off my heels and laid in bed without even changing and fell into a deep slumber until morning.

When I woke up the next day, my head was heavy and slightly pounding from a hangover as I picked myself up from my bed to take a well-needed shower. After my shower, I went out to my living room to finally start opening Larry's gifts. They ranged from shoes, sexy tops, outfits, to a few sexy swimsuits with notes of hoping to see me in them soon. Although my head hurt from the tequila, I was still smiling ear to ear from Larry's sweetness, so I texted him: "I just opened all of the gifts and they are amazing. Thank you, baby. You're so thoughtful. And I see all the sexy swimwear, are we going somewhere?" Within seconds, he responded to my text with "You deserve that and so much more. And I'm not going to give you something sexy to wear and not give you a place to wear it to."

I was smiling from ear to ear. There was nothing that could take me down from this high. Or so I thought. Another few days went by after my birthday when I started to get this unnerving feeling in the bottom of my stomach. For some reason, he wasn't as responsive and his texts read a little differently. Whatever was going on, I knew there had to be a good reason, yet I was acting like he was secretly married or something! In order to clear my head, I had to make the call. Unfortunately, he didn't pick up, so I hung up and just left a voice note via text.

"Hey, listen, I just feel like things are feeling weird right now between us. I don't know if things have changed or what, but just be honest with me and let me know if you decided to be with someone else," I paused, wondering if I was getting too serious for nothing and decided to make a lighthearted joke. "What are you, married?"

I didn't hear back from Larry until the next day when he had a shocking confession to make—because he felt that I wasn't interested in marriage, he had gotten back with an ex-girlfriend! My heart plummeted through my stomach when I read the text the next morning. After having such a lovely week being spoiled for my birthday, how could he suddenly drop this grenade of information on me as if we weren't dating for the last few months already? I couldn't hold in my anger as I called him up to give him a piece of my mind.

"Ava–"

"No, you listen to me. I never told you I wasn't interested in marriage. Where did you get that from? You were just telling me how you would make me breakfast in bed hashtag goals, hashtag birthday dick, sent me all kinds of gifts, and three days later you decided to get back with an ex. Wow!" I shouted and hung up on him.

It took me a few days to calm down from not only the anger but also the hurt. My living room was still filled with his gifts, which only made me more annoyed. Impulsive, I sent him a petty text.

Hey, I'm gonna exchange some of your gifts.

Before you do that, try them on and take a picture to send to me. I really want to see you in them. I miss you, Ava, he replied immediately, which I didn't expect given his new "girlfriend."

You're so confusing, Larry! You're just giving me mixed signals. You just got back together with someone else and now you're saying you miss me?

I'm sorry, but I do really miss you, Ava.

A week after my birthday, I started scrolling through Instagram and noticed a post from Larry's daughter that made my jaw drop immediately: Larry had gotten married the day after my birthday. He didn't just get back with an ex-girlfriend, this negro got married! I dropped my phone in complete shock as everything started playing in my head over and over. I pulled up his contact and sent him a text right away.

Did you get married?

Um, yes, I did, love. Why do you ask...?

Anger boiled under my skin as soon as I saw his reply. "Why'd I ask??" I responded, *"WOW, you're a liar!"* He replied, *You are so black and white. The world has a lot of gray and beige. This is why relationships are difficult for people who operate with absolutes. No human being is perfect.*

I asked myself, did this psycho just gaslight me?? No matter how charming or romantic he was, there was no amount of love left in my heart for this cheating, lying-ass motherfucker. I deleted his number immediately and put all of his gifts straight into the trash. With Larry married and being a complete liar, I wanted nothing to do with him. However, he wasn't out of my life entirely, no matter how much I wanted him to be. His daughter, Rebecca, continued to reach out to me for help with internships and advice. She was so sweet that I didn't want to get my personal relationship with her father in the way of the one we'd built on our own. At first, it was hard talking to her without visualizing him. I would get disgusted. I had to work hard to not take her dad's foolishness out on her.

One day while talking with Rebecca, she mentioned needing documentation from her mother for an internship I'd helped her get, hesitantly, I repeated what she said to make sure I heard her correctly. I heard her just fine! A ringing immediately went through my ears like I'd gone to a rave and hung out by the speakers for too long. I was in shock! I thought to myself, maybe this is an aunt who she now calls her mother, since her mother is deceased. Maybe this person is a mother-figure. I couldn't imagine anyone telling a lie so egregious as this one.

Larry wasn't a widow; he was simply divorced. There was no traumatic sob story about his middle child finding her dead in the kitchen when she was alive and well, living less than an hour away from me. The birthdate he gave me wasn't even real! It was ten days earlier than his real birthday. Everything about that man was a complete scam. My mouth dropped in disbelief as I tried to wrap my head around all of this. He was a lying narcissistic psychopath. Who the hell lied about the mother of their child being dead?!

The only people I turned to after everything fell apart were Leeta and my mother. Leeta, being the Care Bear she was, was always trying to find the silver lining to cheer me up. But my mother gave him no mercy and said she felt sorry for his new wife and was happy that I had dodged a bullet. There was nothing left for that man to say to change my mind anymore after suffering through his pathological lies for so many months.

"What kind of lying ass nig—" Hannah started.

"Hannah, now you know better than to finish that word!" Nina interrupted.

"In this case, he is the N word, and you know I don't mean anything by it. You know I'm not a racist. N words come in all colors!" Hannah tried to explain, but she was completely wrong.

"You are absolutely right, he is one! But now is not the time for us to give you a history lesson. How long have you been around us, around Black people? Your whole damn life! My situation doesn't give you a pass. You're still a little White girl," I laughed at Hannah's ridiculousness. Even as friends, there were definitely boundaries that shouldn't be crossed.

"So, stay in yo' lane!" Leeta chimed in with piercing eyes. Leeta was the non-confrontational one, so to see that "bitch, I'll slap you" look on her face with such a demanding tone shocked all of us, including Hannah. We all burst out laughing, screaming "Dayumm, Leeta!"

We knew Hannah didn't mean anything by it. Hell, we all needed to stop saying the N-word, but again, that still didn't grant my little Hannah Banana a pass. She'd been around us so long that she forgot who she was. Come to think of it, I'd never seen Hannah hanging with other White people, except family and when we were in school. Hannah was my sister, but we still had to check her from time to time.

More Drinks & Recap

I couldn't put into words how relieved I felt now that the spotlight was no longer on me. The other ladies at the table turned back and forth to each other with their snappy commentary still talking about that horrible man, but thankfully no one was looking for more from me. There was only so long I could spend talking about that fool after having to live it myself. I finished the rest of my drink down to the very last drop and let the alcohol relax me.

Slowly, the conversation drifted away from me when Leeta's phone rang on the table. Because of the silly contact photos she put for each of us, it was no surprise to anyone who was calling when a picture of Sidney singing with a mop handle wearing the work uniform from the job we met at popped up. Everyone exchanged silent glances at each other as Leeta hesitated for a moment before picking up the phone. It was all fun and laughs for the last hour or two, but we still had our best friend who needed our help.

"Hey, Sid," Leeta said after answering the phone. Nina whispered in her ear and mouthed the word "speaker" to Leeta so that we could all hear. Leeta nodded her head and set her phone down onto the middle of the table on speaker. We all leaned forward and held our breath as we each tilted one ear closer to hear better.

"Are you guys still at Big Ben's?" Sidney asked. Her voice was tired and a little hoarse, probably from shouting at her no-good, cheating husband. I rolled my eyes as soon as I remembered what he did to my best friend, with heat bubbling in my chest once again.

"Yeah, but I think we might head out soon. Are you okay? We can wait for you," Leeta explained as she looked at us in a circle. Nina nodded her head, agreeing. Between Michael waiting for Nina back home and Hannah's daughter Sara's bedtime coming up soon too, it was about time everyone started heading home. As we waited for Sidney to reply, the sound of muffled cries filled our table. I dropped my gaze to the table as I listened to my best friend try to hide her tears when I knew that her marriage was falling apart. It felt like Alex was personally driving a dagger through my heart and jamming it further and further into my chest with how shitty he treated Sidney. This was the last thing I ever wanted for any of my girlfriends.

"I'll tell you guys more in person, but I'll be okay," Sidney replied with a heavy sigh. She hung up the phone, leaving us all speechless around the table. None of us knew what to say as we all anxiously waited for Sidney's arrival.

"See you soon," Leeta chimed in, but she was too late. The call had already ended. "She's on her way now," Leeta announced as she put her phone away. Even though we could all hear the phone call, returning back to Sidney's entire situation felt so surreal that I actually needed someone to remind me what was going on. Sure, I'd been cheated on by terrible men before, but to have someone turn their back on vows they'd made to love you forever was in an entirely different ballpark than any of the pain and hurt that I'd experienced.

Fifteen minutes later, a puffy-eyed Sidney walked through the front doors of Big Ben's as she looked around for our table. With my seat facing the door, I was the first one to spot her, so I stood up and waved my hand to get her attention. Her face lit up as soon as she saw me and quickly made her way over. Although she looked calm and collected on the outside, there was still great pain brewing behind her eyes that I knew things were not as simple or easy as she tried to make it sound over the phone. I pushed out of my seat and met her halfway to pull her into a large hug. Sidney fell into my arms, but in a much different way compared to this morning when she was waving around a giant knife. She definitely needed my support, but I could tell she wasn't drowning anymore. Sidney tightened her grip around my back as she rested her cheek against my shoulder. A huge part of me wished we could have stayed like that, frozen in time so that I could protect my best friend from all of the damage done to her, so I just held onto her without saying a word.

Sidney was the first to pull back from the hug, waking me back up to reality once again. I looped my arm around hers and guided her to our table. The rest of our friends watched us carefully from afar, anxiously waiting for our arrival. I could especially see Nina antsy in her seat, waiting to check up on Sidney right away.

"Sidney, are you okay?" Nina questioned eagerly the moment we were within arm's reach of the table.

"No," Sidney said flatly as her eyes started to water. "But I will be after a few drinks. Order me whatever y'all have times three," she joked with a small laugh. Sidney sniffled and took her seat with the best smile she could muster up. As soon as she sat down, Nina and Leeta each grabbed one of her hands to give her a squeeze.

We let out a light chuckle along with Sidney. My eyes traveled around the table to see how everyone else was doing. Leeta rested her head on Sidney's shoulder as she rubbed Sidney's arm while Nina was still holding onto Sidney's hand. Before standing up to order Sidney's drinks, Hannah gave her best reassuring smile from across the table, as she wasn't sitting close enough to Sidney compared to Leeta and Nina. Despite all of us doing our best to be there for Sidney, none of us had ever been in this kind of situation before, so all we could do was play everything by ear. We didn't know whether to laugh or to cry. We weren't sure what was comforting or triggering. However, the best we knew we could do was just be there for Sidney in whatever way she needed, because that was what best friends were for.

When Hannah came back from the bar, there was a light rumble that made her pause and blush. I looked at her and then down at her stomach before cracking up.

"Are you starving yourself or something, Hannah?" I cried out at the sound of her stomach grumbling.

"It's been a long day!" Hannah retorted playfully as she took her seat and swatted my shoulder.

"We should get some food since all we've had are drinks!" Leeta added as she popped her head up from Sidney's shoulder with a big smile.

"Alright, let's look at this menu," I announced as I grabbed the laminated paper from beside me and set it in the middle of the table so everyone could see. Shortly after we started looking over the menu, we started to realize how hungry we all were, drinking on empty stomachs. Our hungry eyes settled on four different appetizers, including a sharing platter, and another round of drinks.

As we waited for our food and drinks to arrive, all of our attention naturally drifted back to Sidney. She stared back at us with another heavy sigh before looking down at her lap.

"I know you guys are looking for answers, and I said I would update you, but I just can't talk about myself right now. Maybe once I get a few drinks in me I'll feel okay enough to talk, but for now, can we just focus on something else?" Sidney confessed with her head down, still avoiding eye contact with us. Since she wasn't able to see any of us with her gaze on her lap, I darted my eyes around the table telepathically urging someone to talk about something to keep Sidney's mind off of her own troubles. After talking for the last hour about the hurricane that was Lying-Ass Larry, I was already burnt out, so the last thing I wanted to do was pick up another conversation. I nudged Hannah with my elbow to say something as she texted on her phone under the table. Her body shook from the surprise as she snapped her head up and redirected her attention to the table.

"Huh?" she accidentally said. "What?" She looked around the table with confusion as she tried to catch up on the conversation.

"Ava," Sidney interrupted at the same moment. With her head still hung low, she innocently asked, "So what in the world is going on with Larry?"

In that moment, my heart stopped. Partly from shock that after everything that went down with her husband in the last hour, she still remembered someone as irrelevant as Larry and partly from the thought of having to relive that entire story a second time in a row. My mouth dropped and I was unable to speak. Sidney always had a special way of leaving me speechless, but this was definitely a first.

"I'd be lying if I said I was excited to retell you that entire story, but honestly I don't know if I have the mental capacity to go through his lying ass two times in a row," I laughed apologetically to Sidney. Instantly, Hannah's eye's lit up like fireworks on the Fourth of July as she perked up in her seat and folded her hands neatly on the table.

"Don't worry, Sid. If Ava doesn't want to tell you, I got you." Hannah exclaimed as our food and drinks all arrived at once. "Perfect timing! Girrrrrllllllll, let me tell you, it was definitely a rollercoaster," she began with great excitement as she chugged a huge gulp of her drink, which only left me even more speechless than before. But if it meant that I didn't have to tell that crazy story a second time, I was not opposed to Hannah's version. I sat back in my seat and closed my eyes for a brief second to rest my mind before watching Hannah's chaotic storytelling unfold. A huge smile wiped across Sidney's face as she finally had a temporary getaway from her own troubles.

"So, as you know, Larry was just some guy that Ava was dating for six months. Things were looking good, repeat dates and all, but the thing was that they were long distance. This guy was constantly visiting from Texas. Texas!" Hannah's eyes bugged out as she emphasized where he lived.

Dating long distance was never something that she understood because she was the kind of girl who needed to have someone within reach at any given time, so the fact that I dated someone across state lines damn near blew her mind. Leeta and Nina giggled at Hannah's silliness, but I knew that Hannah was being completely serious. I watched as Sidney's eyes grew more and more interested in the story. Although Hannah had a way of exaggerating certain details based on what she personally thought was more interesting instead of what was actually important to the story, she definitely had a way of reeling people into a story like no one else I knew.

"So, after having sex, Ava's trying to get to know him, right? And of all things, he tells her that the mother of his kids is DEAD!" Hannah shouted as she threw her hands into the air. Sidney gasped at the sound of death with eyes filled with worry as she stared back at Hannah intensely, obviously oblivious to why Hannah made it such a dramatic gesture.

"Ugh," Nina scoffed as she shook her head, causing Sidney great confusion when the story sounded like it was supposed to be serious and sad. "Just keep listening," Nina advised as she waved off Sidney's concern.

"So, Lying-Ass Larry was saying all this smooth shit like 'do you want to fall in love' and trying to sweet talk our Ava, and homegirl here was actually falling for it!" Hannah sat back in her seat and crossed her arms as she shook her head in my direction. This caused Sidney to follow suit and look in my direction too.

"Okay, I was not some kind of sucker or something!" I cried out in defense as I elbowed Hannah gently, but she simply turned her head away from me with a playful scoff.

"It's my turn to tell the story, not you," Hannah stated as she held up the hand in my face. My mouth dropped at her audacity.

"It's literally my life story," I muttered as I took a sip of my drink. Leeta and Nina started cracking up at Hannah and my banter, which made it clear how many years we'd known each other. Sisters often bickered and argued, which was exactly what my relationship with Hannah was like, but it was only a further testament of how close we were.

"Anyway, Ava was telling him she wants to fall in love cause she thought he was something and then out of nowhere, he ghosts her!" Hannah shouted with bugged out eyes as if this was her first time hearing the story herself. Sidney gasped and covered her mouth with her hands like she was watching a horror movie. All I could do was shake my head at the chaos that was ensuing.

"What!" Sidney cried out as she ping ponged her gaze between Hannah and me, trying to process the story.

"Mmhm," Leeta nodded her head.

I couldn't believe how this entire day suddenly got turned onto me and my love life. As much as I loved Sidney and wanted to help her heal in whatever way she needed, I didn't expect it all to happen at my own expense! Couldn't we talk about anyone other than me right now? Sidney was lucky I loved her like family, or else there was no way I would allow myself to be stuck in this situation TWICE.

"This went on and off for a bit until he finally apologized, and can you believe she forgave him?! Then, on Ava's birthday, he started showering her with gifts and trying to basically win her back. And she fell for ALL of it!" Hannah exclaimed like I was the biggest fool in the history of love to have ever existed. A few other customers nearby our table turned around to stare, which only made me want to hide under the table. Listening to Hannah, all I could do was roll my eyes and sigh in complete embarrassment. Of course, there was truth to what she was saying, but I wasn't that naive or dumb in love!

"But what happens next? HE GETS BACK WITH HIS EX!" Hannah said even louder.

At that point, she might as well just stand up on her seat and tell the entire bar with how loud she was talking. I wasn't one to normally be easily embarrassed, but Hannah was another species when it came to second-hand embarrassment because of how shameless she was willing to act in public. It was something I hated and admired at the same time. On one hand, I commended her for always being true to herself no matter who was watching, but on the other hand I was usually the one with her, which made people stare at me just as much.

"WHAT!" Sidney nearly fell out of her seat from the shock as she threw her head back.

Hannah stood up and slammed her hands on the table as she said for dramatic effect, "While he was dating Ava, he was engaged and living with someone else. Our girl got PLAYED!"

"Damn shame" Nina shook her head as she rubbed Sidney's shoulder.

"Oh my god, Hannah," I gasped as I dropped my head and tried to cover my face with my hands from the rest of the bar. I could swear damn near everyone was watching now.

"A day after her birthday, this fool got MARRIED!" Hannah smacked the table once again, causing the manager to turn in our direction.

"WHAAAT!"

"Then Ava starts getting even closer to his oldest daughter, who lays the biggest news on her," Hannah paused for the ultimate dramatic effect. She inched her finger at Sidney, signaling to her to come closer. Sidney leaned closer with eager ears for the final kicker of the story.

"The ex-wife was never dead. He literally faked her death just to tell Ava some sob story!" Hannah threw her hands in the air as she plopped back into her seat like she'd just finished running a marathon.

Sidney's mouth fell to the ground and stayed there for a long time as she tried to make sense of the whirlwind that was Lying-Ass Larry. It was hilarious to me that everyone was having such a hard time hearing the story when I was the one who actually had to live it. It was one of the biggest shockers of my life, but I was still able to get through it. Yet, somehow, based on how much this was affecting Sidney, it didn't look like everyone was gonna get through it like I did.

"Holy shit, Ava, and I thought I was bad at picking guys!" Sidney cried out. I opened my mouth to fight back but held my tongue as I knew better than to say something.

"Hey, I'm past it, so all I can do is keep moving forward," I shrugged with a heavy sigh.

"You're right. No matter what happens, we just have to keep moving forward," Sidney agreed as she nodded her head and took a drink. We could all see Sidney's shift in demeanor and knew something big was coming, so we remained quiet and waited for her to make the next move. She took a few deep breathes and mouthed something to herself before folding her hands neatly on the table.

"So, regarding me and Alex…" she started as she cleared her throat and got comfortable in her seat. "We're getting divorced. Yay," Sidney announced flatly. It was so sarcastic that it sounded just like when she first told us she was getting married to Alex seventeen years ago.

A ripple effect of surprise ran through the table as the news hit each of us. It hit Nina first, who was always the first to judge, whether or not it was for good reason. She opened her mouth to make a snappy comment, but Leeta shot her a look, which made her remain silent. Leeta was next, but she went straight into mom mode and comforted Sidney with a warm hug instead of words. Next was Hannah.

"Oh my god," Hannah gasped without any sensitivity. She recoiled in her seat as she whispered the word "divorce" quietly to herself.

"Are you okay, Sidney?" I asked when the news finally sunk in for me. After being with her since yesterday when she first confessed the news of Alex's affair, I would have never guessed this was how everything was going to unfold. Not that I ever expected Sidney to stick around with a cheating man, but hearing it officially from Sidney's mouth was still huge news.

"I was the one who proposed the idea. Funnily enough, he didn't even try to contest it. Ultimately, it isn't as sad as I thought it would be, just mostly shock. I thought Alex was going to be my forever, but life just has other plans for us, you know?" Sidney finally confessed in a serious tone, no sarcasm to be found. That's what made the entire situation even more sad: Sidney was genuinely crushed by all of it. She was always the nonchalant, let me mask all of my feelings with jokes kind of person, so to see her willingly be openly vulnerable was an incredibly rare sight even for us, her best friends.

"I'm glad you're taking it so well, Sid," Hannah said comfortingly as she reached across the table to place her hand on top of Sidney's.

"You know who's taking it the best? Alex," Sidney replied with a chuckle. "Honestly, I think it was just a weight lifted off of his shoulders." She shrugged her shoulders and played with her straw mindlessly.

"What are you talking about? You weren't some burden or something. You're the best he could even dream of tying down. It's a miracle he even did," Nina angrily argued. Her mama bear tendencies were starting to come out as she balled her hands into fists, probably wishing they were around Alex's neck right now.

"So…" Sidney started as she sat up straight in her seat. "Alex is actually in love with another woman."

"Are you serious?" I questioned in disbelief. More than the shock of Alex being in love with another woman—that lying, cheating rat of a man—but I couldn't believe how calm Sidney was being about all of this. If he'd been my man of almost twenty years, seventeen of them being marriage, and being the father of my children, I would have made sure there was hell to pay if he crossed me like this.

"Is it the woman he has the child with?" Hannah inquired curiously. I slapped her arm with the back of my hand to remind her not to push Sidney to talk about anything more than she was comfortable with. Hannah gave me a mean glare at first from the slap until she realized her mistake and mouthed "oh" to me.

"The funny thing is, I thought that too," Sidney laughed. It was a little scary how calmly she was handling all of this, so we all remained still as we tried to navigate how to best go about the conversation.

"What do you mean?" Leeta asked carefully.

"I thought the woman he was in love with was the girl he knocked up, but you know what? It's not," Sidney's laughter turned into hysterical cackling with cry-laughing tears streaming down her face. All of us sat rigid in our seats, a little afraid of Sidney being on the verge of yet another emotional breakdown. She wiped her eyes with the back of her hands with a huge smile on her face. Especially after her breakdown with the cleaver this morning, this was quite the terrifying sight. Instinctually, I checked around the table for any knives, but they were all still wrapped up in our napkins.

"So, there's another woman involved," Hannah repeated in plain words. It was more so for her own sake to understand the situation than to ask Sidney.

"Bingo," Sidney replied as she pointed at Hannah like she'd just correctly answered a question on a game show. "She's a totally different woman. He was telling me how they met one day while he was away on a business trip and instantly clicked in a way he felt we hadn't for a really long time. I mean, if you asked me, I thought we were perfectly fine, but I guess I'm not as exciting as some young, social media "celebrity"…" Her voice drifted as she gritted her teeth and muttered under breath.

"He showed you a picture?" Nina said flatly with her mouth open.

The audacity of men these days…

"He was basically trying to sell me on the idea of this woman," Sidney explained as she picked up her drink and chugged the rest of it in a flash. She slammed the empty cup on the table and grabbed Nina's drink for more.

"That man has damn near lost his mind," Leeta scolded with a heavy pout.

The rest of us didn't know what to say anymore, as Sidney's

situation only continued to get worse. It was bad enough he had a secret baby but to have two women on the side on top of being a married father of two? Who did Alex think he was? Fabio in a romance novel from the 1990s? If that's what he thought of himself to reason his infidelity with all of these women, the man needed a rude awakening.

"So, divorce was just the thing that made the most sense for us. I deserve better than that, and, apparently, he gets to run into the sunset with his future child bride." Sidney continued to laugh with a blank stare until her voice quieted down and real tears started to pool in her eyes once again.

Hannah and I got up from our seats to rub her shoulders as Leeta and Nina gave her hugs from each side while our heartbroken Sidney violently sobbed in the center. We stayed there for a while before Sidney's crying started to let up. After we sat back down, Hannah was the first to speak up.

"I know it hurts like crazy right now, but this is honestly for the better. You don't need trash like that," Nina said as she tried to reassure our friend. It didn't seem like any of our words were really getting through to Sidney, but it was all we could do to help.

"You're so much better than him," Leeta added as she gave Sidney another squeeze.

"What an asshole," Hannah scoffed irately as she rolled her eyes. Sidney's eyes perked up at Hannah's comment. She smirked and nodded her head. It was the first time she was responding to anything we said, so I decided to chime in as well.

"Yeah, he's an asshole!" I cried out and took a heavy drink of my margarita. It looked like it was slowly lifting Sidney's spirit hearing us trash her husband, so we continued to scream and curse as our third round of drinks were finally kicking in. As Nina and I got riled up, I noticed from the corner of my eye that Hannah pulled out her phone again under the table, but I was too preoccupied to think much of it when the manager of the bar came over to our table.

"Excuse me ladies, but I'm gonna need you all to keep it down. You're disturbing other customers," the manager gently requested.

"What is up with men always trying to tell us what to do when they ain't shit?" Nina argued to the table, completely ignoring the manager's presence. I gave him an apologetic smile and nodded in agreement that we would try to keep it down. He stepped away, but there was no promise from everyone else at the table of silence or compliance.

"Fuck that! You do what you want and say what you want!" Hannah agreed as she cheered Nina noisily. Their drinks splashed out of their cups and down their hands from their messy cheers.

"ALEX YOU ASSHOLE!" Sidney screamed at the top of her lungs. It was like watching a balloon deflate after being filled with helium for days. She was finally releasing her steam, and I was so relieved—screaming was much healthier than threatening men with a cleaver.

"You tell him, Sid!" Leeta cheered as she threw her arm in the air with her drink as well.

"Ladies, this is your second warning. Please calm down, I urge you to be mindful of other customers," the manager repeated a second time as he returned to our table.

"Yeah, yeah," Nina replied as she waved him off. He gave me a weird look but I just drunkenly shrugged my shoulders. Nina had a point that men were always trying to tell us what to do, so I couldn't argue with her on that!

As the bar manager walked away, the odd looks from the other tables finally started to register to all of us as we remembered we were in a public place. I guess the drinks took effect during our rage drunk phase, but somehow we made our way onto sadness. As I finished my drink, Nina was suddenly in tears as she held onto Sidney and rubbed her back. The two held onto each other, as Leeta was away in the restroom and Hannah was texting on her phone secretly yet again.

Surprises Just Keep Comin'

By the time we finished our fourth drink, Sidney had fully caught up to us but in a fraction of the time. She swayed in her seat as she sat with her eyes half shut. Leeta was bobbing her head up and down as she rocked to the music playing in the background. Nina was looking over the menu, contemplating whether or not to get anything more to drink. Then there was Hannah, who was still on her phone secretly under the table. I wanted to confront her about it, because what was more important than helping our best friend, but potentially starting an argument didn't seem like the most helpful thing to do in this situation. So I simply sat back and watched everyone as I giggled softly to myself behind my margarita glass.

"You guys are right," Sidney said with a slurred voice as she raised her empty glass. "I don't need him."

"You don't, Sid!" I agreed and clinked my empty glass with hers.

"I am great," she drunkenly said as she squinted her eyes and looked around the table.

"He doesn't know what he's missing out on," Leeta chimed in.

As we all cheered Sidney on, Hannah was the only one remaining quiet. She kept glancing at the front door and then back at her phone suspiciously. Perhaps it was the four drinks in my system, but I could feel my self-control starting to dwindle away the more I saw Hannah ignoring the rest of the table. She had already privately taken a phone call with her mother to help put her daughter to sleep tonight, so what exactly was so important that she needed to keep checking her phone? There was nothing I could think of, so she left me with no other choice.

"Hannah, what is going on?" I finally confronted. My voice came out a little more harsh than I intended, which made everyone quiet down from the seriousness in my voice.

"What do you mean?" she questioned innocently.

"You keep checking your phone, and now you can't stop staring at the door. Are you waiting for a Tinder date to walk in or something?" I scoffed.

"No, that's not it. I just," Hannah started before she stopped herself. She paused to gather herself before taking a deep breath. "There's something I've been keeping from you guys."

"Oh no, here we go again. Another secret? I don't know how many we can take today," Leeta cried out with worry.

"No, it's a good thing! Or at least I hope so…" Hannah tried to comfort, but her own uncertainty made us all more concerned about what she was going to say.   "So… I've been dating someone for almost a year now." As soon as she said the words, she shut her eyes tight, afraid to see what our reactions were.

"OMG!" We all burst out in unison. All four of our mouths collectively dropped onto the table. None of us had any idea of what to say to an announcement like that.

"And I want you guys to finally meet him," Hannah continued, as she peeked through one open eye. Once she saw that everything was okay and none of us were upset, she opened her other eye and shrugged her shoulders.

"How did you keep this from us for a whole YEAR?" Nina shouted with great emphasis on year. It was the question on all of our minds, so I was secretly thankful that Nina was unfiltered enough to be the one to say it on all of our behalf.

"I think things are getting pretty serious, so it finally felt right to bring him. I know with everything with Sidney isn't ideal, but at the same time I figured why not for a change of mood right now, you know?" Hannah explained as she clutched her phone in her hands tightly. She had a nervous smile as she waited for our reactions to her big news.

As always, Hannah had the craziest timing for things. She chimed in with smart-mouthed comments when it was least helpful, she remembered the things you wanted the group to forget, and now she dropped life-changing secrets like it was no big deal. After being single for so many years, this was the last thing I expected, yet somehow I was right once again. Was I clairvoyant or something? First Lying-Ass Larry being married and now Hannah with a new man? At this rate, I needed to just quit my job and become a psychic!

"How... how?" Nina stuttered, unable to get the words out of her mouth. She seemed to be going through the most aggressive shock out of the four of us. Hannah just shrugged her shoulders yet again, as if she didn't just drop a truth bomb just as big as everyone else had.

"Leeta, you don't have anything you're hiding from us, right? I don't know if we can take another secret," I asked as I looked over at her, also blinded by Hannah's news.

"No! Nothing from me. You know I always tell you guys everything!" Leeta replied cheerfully. Of the four of us, she was certainly the least affected by Hannah's news and seemed to have already recovered.

"How did you hide a whole human for a year?" Nina cried out after she was finally able to collect her thoughts. She shook her head in disbelief as we watched the gears in her brain try to process Hannah and a stable man that she wanted us to meet.

"Yeah, talk about secrets. That's the pot calling the kettle black," I chimed in sarcastically.

"It's been difficult for me too, okay?" Hannah threw her hands in the air before covering her face. The four of us exchanged worried glances before scooting closer to Hannah to figure out what exactly was so wrong. Hannah had a way of being extra and dramatic, but when things got serious, we knew that she wasn't exaggerating.

"What's wrong?" We all asked together softly. Hannah tried to muffle a few sniffles, which only made us more worried. Hannah was not a crier. Not after her long-term college boyfriend broke up with her or when her baby daddy left her, and definitely not when she became a single mom for Sara. So, to see Hannah even shed one tear, we knew that this was really affecting her much more than we originally anticipated.

"Look, I know at times I act like I forget I'm White, and, admittedly, I do, because you guys are my best friends, but I still listen to what you guys tell me, especially when it comes to being Black," Hannah mumbled behind her hands as she tried to control her crying.

"What are you talking about?" I questioned gently as I put my arm around my Hannah Banana.

"I just-- I've heard you guys joke but not really joke about how all Black men want are 'other' women now and how frustrated it made you guys. I didn't know how to admit that I was becoming one of those 'other' women," she finally confessed. Her voice broke off at the end of her sentence as she started to really cry. Tears fell onto her lap, which only broke my heart even more. "I really do make an effort to understand where you guys are coming from, even if sometimes I forget to show it…"

It wasn't often that Hannah was real with us on a heart-to-heart level like this, so it was a big surprise to see her this way. But more than that, my heart ached to hear her say these things, especially after how long I'd known her.

"Wait, he's Black? He better not be fine," Sidney jumped in with a lighthearted joke to help brighten up the mood at the table. It took me some time, but it wasn't until Sidney's comment that it fully registered with me what Hannah had just said. Not only was she hiding a man for a whole year, but she was hiding a Black man from us! Immediately, Leeta and Nina burst out laughing, but for me it wasn't funny. I looked up at Hannah with only disappointment, and I knew that she could see it all over my face.

"See? That's exactly why I didn't say anything," Hannah groaned.

"Look, Hannah, I'm not disappointed he's Black. I'm disappointed that you seriously thought you couldn't tell us or introduce him to us. Damn, Hannah! We all talk trash and joke around with one another—" I tried to explain, but it seemed that the issue was even deeper than we understood, because Hannah interrupted me with the saddest eyes.

"No, but that's not how it is though!" Hannah erupted. "After you hear the same 'joke' over and over, it no longer feels like a joke anymore." She pouted and pounded the last of her drink.

No one at the table had anything to say in response. Although we were used to being rough with each other, especially knowing each other for so long, we had to admit that Hannah did have a point. Being Black women, we never had to think about how Hannah felt as not only the only White woman in our friend group but also as the only non-Black woman. The more Hannah's words sunk in, a wave of shock, sadness, and embarrassment all morphed into one washed over each and every one of us, and we all hung our heads down in shame. Regardless of race, the bigger picture at hand was that we had all let our best friend down to the point that she didn't even feel comfortable to be honest with us. That wasn't what being best friends was about, and it was on us to admit that.

"Hannah, we're so sorry we made you feel that way. I know we like to joke a lot about love and how hard dating is, but we never want how we feel to affect you and your relationships," Leeta started to apologize.

"Yeah, exactly. At the end of the day, all men are the same anyway," Sidney remarked, clearly making a dig at her own soon-to-be ex-husband.

"We just hope that the man you've found is good to you and knows how to love you the way you deserve to be loved. That's all we want for you, that's all we want for any of us," I said as I gave her a tight squeeze around her shoulders.

"Thanks, everyone. I know you guys mean well at the end of the day, but this was just something really hard for me to deal with. But I really hope you guys like him," Hannah finally had her light back as she flashed a worried smile. She pressed her hands together in a praying motion under her chin as she buzzed with nervousness.

"He better be damn good if you've kept him a secret for a whole year!" Nina cackled, still unable to let go about how long Hannah kept the secret.

"Show us his Instagram! I don't remember you posting anyone on yours," Sidney exclaimed as she tried to reach for Hannah's phone.

Hannah opened her phone and pulled up his account. His name was Devin, and boy was he fine! I eyed Hannah with surprise after seeing her man. His page was filled with pictures of him and Hannah from the last year. He seemed to be a frequent poster, with a new picture of the two of them from just a few days ago. It was really sweet to see how proud he was to show Hannah off publicly, but it made me wonder why Hannah never posted a picture of him back.

"That's so cute he has so many pictures of you guys together! Ain't no way any woman gonna mistaken him for a single man," Sidney cheered bittersweetly.

"How come you've never posted him? Aside from not wanting to tell us," Nina questioned curiously.

"I dunno. You guys know I don't post often in the first place. I just didn't feel like it was necessary. Even if you guys know, I probably wouldn't post us anyway," Hannah replied.

I nodded my head in agreement as I listened to her explanation. This was something Hannah and I both were on the same page about. I also wasn't someone who needed to let everyone on social media know about my personal business. It didn't mean that I loved my partner any less if I posted or didn't post them on my socials. All that mattered was how we felt in our relationship and having that security ourselves, not based on the opinions of others online.

"I don't blame you. I normally don't post either, but with a man like Devin, I might change my mind," I joked as I nudged Hannah with my shoulder playfully. This seemed to cheer her up as she giggled and relaxed her shoulders a bit.

"I wonder what he's like. Pictures aren't enough!" Nina whined as she handed Hannah back her phone.

"I guess you're about to find out," Hannah said with a big smile on her face as she looked over at the front doors. She waved her hand and cried out, "Devin! Over here!" Hannah jumped up out of her seat and danced her way to a six-foot-three, tall chocolate man with a beautiful, chiseled face gazing only at Hannah in a busy bar full of customers. He swooped her up in his arms and swung her around in the middle of the bar as if they were living in their own fairytale together. Hannah's face lit up like lights on Christmas day as they touched foreheads together like no one was watching—except we were most certainly watching. From the moment he walked through the doors to the beaming smiles on both of their faces as they took a seat at our table, there was no doubt how much in love they were. I couldn't stop smiling just watching them!

"Hello, ladies, my name is Devin," he introduced himself as he shook each of our hands.

"H-hi," Sidney stuttered with a gaping mouth as she looked up at Devin like he was some kind of chocolate god. Nina nudged Sidney with her elbow, causing Sidney to wince and smile shyly.

"Pleased to meet you. This is Nina, Sidney, Ava, and I'm Leeta," Leeta replied calmly on our behalf.

"It's been a long time coming, but I'm glad we can finally meet," he chuckled with a low voice that made all of us melt a little.

"I can't believe you kept this fine of a man from me!" I hissed in Hannah's ear as I pulled her back and cupped my hand over her ear. "But I'm super happy for you!"

Hannah giggled girlishly in a way I'd never seen before, despite knowing her for most of my life. It warmed my heart to watch her this way, especially knowing how heartbroken she'd been so many times in the past. After breaking up with her long-term college boyfriend and then being left behind by her baby daddy, Hannah had stayed out of dating for a really long time to avoid getting hurt again. But seeing her blushing now with the way Devin looked at her like she was the most beautiful woman he'd ever laid his eyes on, I knew that he was going to be a keeper right away.

We spent about thirty minutes talking to Devin, and one by one, we were all falling for him in our own way. He was sweet, funny, and one of the biggest gentlemen I'd seen in a very long time. Where did Hannah find this man, and did he have a brother?! No matter how many questions we grilled him on, he kept a smile on his face and answered everything without a single complaint. Devin kept his arm wrapped around Hannah's shoulders, keeping her warm as he spoke.

When it was almost time for closing, our server came by with our bill and placed it on the table beside Nina. However, before Nina could even finish looking at the bill, Devin whipped out his credit card and handed the bill back to the server immediately.

"You didn't need to do that! The bill was $301.68!" Nina gasped.

"Don't worry about it. My treat for spending part of your evening with me, ladies," he replied as he stood up with Hannah still in his arm and pulled out forty dollars to leave as a tip on the table. I watched Nina and Sidney exchange looks at each other, fully impressed at how generous Hannah's boyfriend was.

We all pushed out of our seats and gathered our belongings as we began sobering up, when Devin turned to Hannah with his hands fidgeting at his sides. She stopped to stare at him in confusion, which caught my attention.

"Is everything okay, Devin?" Hannah whispered quietly.

"Everything is more than okay, Hannah. I was going to wait until we got home, but something about this moment just feels right. Of course, I never expected it to be in a place like Big Ben's, but I want to do this for you right now in front of your best friends," Devin confessed with a bright smile on his face as he tried to keep his hands still.

"Devin, what are you talking about?" Hannah looked at him confused.

In that moment, everything started moving in slow motion. The bar coincidentally switched onto soft jazz music as they got ready for closing when Devin reached into his jacket pocket and pulled out a bright-red, velvet box with gold finishing. He dropped down onto one knee in front of Hannah, who gasped with her hands over her mouth. Tears instantly filled her eyes as she started breathing heavily in anticipation. Devin slowly opened the box to the biggest diamond ring I'd ever seen in my life. Even in the dim bar lighting, the ring sparkled as the brightest thing in the room—aside from Hannah's beaming smile.

"Oh my God, oh my God," she uttered like a broken record, unable to process the ring.

"Hannah, I know that we've only been dating for one year, and this is not exactly how I pictured the moment we decided to spend the rest of our lives together, but anytime I'm with you is always right. There's still so much I have to learn about you, but I want to spend the rest of my life by your side finding out. You are a beautiful, courageous, and loving mother, and there is nothing more I want than to make you my wife. I promise to make you the happiest woman on earth, if you'll have me. Hannah, will you marry me?" Devin recited, clearly having spent a long time preparing his speech.

"I don't know what to say," Hannah breathed, still in shock.

"Say yes, of course!" Nina hissed at her side.

"Oh, right! Yes, of course, Devin, yes!" Hannah cried out as she jumped with joy.

Relief washed over Devin as he let out a nervous laugh. He pulled out the enormous diamond ring from the box and carefully slipped it onto Hannah's finger. Devin stood up, towering over our tiny Hannah, and held her cheeks softly in his hands before dipping his head for a kiss with his now fiancé.

A roar of applause filled the room, startling all of us, as no one anticipated the rest of the bar to be watching Hannah and Devin's impromptu proposal. There was whistling and cheering from all corners of the room as everyone congratulated the newly engaged couple. A man in the back even shouted "GO, HANNAH," despite being a total stranger.

"Let us see the ring!" Nina shouted eagerly as she reached out for Hannah's hand.

"She means congratulations," I translated to Devin with a chuckle.

"But I also mean show me the ring!" Nina corrected as she held up Hannah's hand in the dim lighting to see all angles of the ring. "Oh my God, Hannah. Damn, that's at least five carats!" All of our mouths flew open at the thought of a five-carat ring. Then Sidney burst out into tears, crying hysterically, but this time without the heartbreak. Devin turned to look at Sidney with great confusion, as he wasn't sure what that meant.

"Don't mind me, it's all just so beautiful," she mumbled in between her congratulatory sobbing.

"Oh, thank God. I thought you were taking back your blessing," Devin joked as he patted Sidney on the shoulder and handed her a napkin from the table.

"Of course not. I know we just met you, but I have a really good feeling about you," Sidney grinned sweetly before lowering her tone and looking at him with a grave expression. "But trust and believe if you dare hurt her, I will come after you with a cleaver."

"Don't worry, I'll take good care of Hannah," Devin chuckled, unaware of how serious Sidney was being.

"No, seriously, you don't want to see Sidney with a cleaver," I clarified.

"Oh," he said, taken back with a frightened look.

"Moving on from knife threats, guys, I'm finally engaged!" Hannah cut in to keep the mood up.

It felt like such a surreal moment to see one of us finally get engaged after all of this time, but it felt so good knowing that Hannah was finally in the hands of a good man. After everything that happened with Alex and Lying-Ass Larry, I couldn't have been happier for my best friend to have finally found the person she belonged with. It even gave me hope that I would find my perfect person one day too.

The Wind-Down

After the cheering and congratulations at Big Ben's ended, we gathered our things and exited the bar with high spirits and the feeling of love in the air. No matter how many times I thought about it, I couldn't believe that my Hannah Banana was finally getting married! Ever since we were young, Hannah was never someone who overly romanticized love or marriage, yet she was one of the most loyal partners I'd ever seen. Somehow, men always found a way to take advantage of her faithfulness and hurt her, but judging off of this one encounter with Devin, I finally felt at ease that my best friend was finally going to get the love and care that she always deserved.

When we made our way to the parking lot, the sky was completely dark after spending hours at Big Ben's. With the exception of Sidney, who started drinking way later than the rest of us, we were all sober enough to safely drive home.

"Did you drive here?" I asked Devin.

"No, I told him to take an Uber so we could go home together," Hannah replied instead. As soon as I heard those words, my heart sank. I was really looking forward to having a talk with Hannah about everything. Although we wouldn't be able to properly talk face to face or even sit in the same car together, I was hoping we could talk on the phone as we drove home. As the only one who knew Hannah since we were teens, I felt like there was a bigger duty and loyalty as her best friend to address the whole secrecy issue about her relationship. More than anything, I just really wanted to talk to her about my feelings privately now that I'd had more time to process everything that went on.

I could understand wanting to keep things secret. Look at me, I did the same about Larry, so it would have been hypocritical of me to say she had to tell me about all of the relationships in her life or that I deserved to know—because that wasn't the case. What truly bothered me was how she must have felt when she thought she needed to keep everything private from us, especially me. Hannah was the closest I'd ever, and would ever, have to a sister, and so I wanted to better understand what we could both do better to improve our relationship to avoid something like this happening again. I had this whole speech ready in my head, but after finding out that Devin was going to be with Hannah, there was no way I was going to be able to talk about something that so heavily involved him in front of him. I had no other choice but to keep my mouth shut, yet again, until we had a better time to talk. Clearing my throat, I tried to put on my best brave face and give my best friend a hug that I could only hope would communicate how sorry I felt putting her through that.

"It was so nice meeting you all," Devin said as he shook our hands one last time.

"Please take care of our girl," Leeta replied as we remained huddled on the sidewalk.

Hannah and Devin waved to us as they headed toward her car holding hands together. Their arms swung as they looked at each other instead of paying attention to where they were going like young puppy love on the school playground. Hannah gave a little leap of joy as she looked at her hand again, and remembered she was now engaged.

"So, we're just gonna go home now?" Sidney shouted as she watched Hannah and Devin leave.

"Who's going to take her home?" Nina questioned as she leaned toward Leeta and I and away from Sidney for privacy.

"You should go home and talk to Michael. I can take her home," Leeta offered.

"No, Leeta, I'll do it. I feel like since it started with me, it's only right that I finish the job. Plus, my place has more room anyway, so it'll be more comfortable for both of us if she stays with me," I suggested as I tried to keep Sidney upright with one arm. She threw my arm off and tried to walk, but the strength in her legs was rapidly dwindling after so many drinks.

"Are you sure, Ava?" Leeta asked, worried.

"I don't think you want to share a bed with that," I whispered as I pointed to a completely obliterated Sidney who was trying to do a sobriety test on herself by walking in a straight line and failing miserably.

"Thank you," Leeta mouthed.

"Alright, Sid, you're coming with me," I announced as I grabbed her arm to stop her from anymore walking.

"I don't want to go home," she whined like a child begging to stay up past her bedtime "Can I stay at your place?" She looked up at me with puppy eyes.

"You got it," I replied as I put her arm around my shoulder so we could make our way to my car.

"I just can't go back there. Alex is probably in our bed with his future child bride," she cried out into the empty parking lot.

"Let's just get your car back first and figure out the rest later," I said as I shushed her.

Sidney nodded her head like a little child as I wrapped my arm around her waist and guided her to my car. I wobbled my way across the pavement as I tried to keep Sidney walking in a straight line. She was still coherent enough to keep herself up, but she was constantly losing her footing and tripping over her own feet that it was no different than walking a toddler the size of a full-grown woman. Leeta and Nina followed beside me within arm's length, ready to catch me or Sidney at any given moment. Originally, Leeta wanted to help carry Sidney on her other side, but Sidney refused to let two of us carry her, as she was certain she was "not that drunk."

We arrived at my car after a few minutes with the help of Nina grabbing my car keys from my purse and Leeta opening the front passenger side door for me. I tried to lay Sidney down on the seat as carefully as I could, but she was so heavy that I lost my grip and she fell back with a low thud. She giggled like a little girl at the mishap until her head tilted onto the armrest and she started to doze off. I shut the door behind her as softly as I could to huddle with Leeta and Nina at the trunk of my car.

"It only took her a few seconds, but it looks like she's knocked out cold now," I whispered as I took one more glance over my shoulder to look in Sidney's direction.

"What a relief," Leeta sighed.

"Now that Sidney is handled, what do we do about Hannah?" I

questioned as I chewed on the corner of my lip, still unable to move past the unresolved parts with our friend.

"What do you mean?" Nina looked at me, puzzled.

"I just feel really guilty for making her feel like she couldn't even share her happiest relationship with us," I explained and folded my arms.

"I still can't believe how she was able to keep a fine man like Devin secret for a whole year. I definitely would have cracked after a few months," Nina commented.

"I know it was our fault for making her feel that way, but I still wish that she would have just come and talked to us. Even if it was just one of us," I shrugged my shoulders in disappointment.

"All we can do now is be better moving forward and learn to communicate better with each other. Just because we're best friends doesn't mean that we're immune to feeling hurt or sad or disappointed by each other. That's just a part of life and friendship," Nina told me as she rubbed my shoulder, noticing how clearly upset I was about this.

"You're right, Nina. I just still can't believe all of this. I wanted to talk to her so bad on the drive home, but it'll just have to wait until another time," I sighed deeply.

"Not to mention you have even bigger problems on your hands," Leeta said as she cocked her head toward drunk Sidney in my car.

Despite Leeta's joke, I still couldn't deny what I was feeling in my heart. One side of me was filled with hurt and guilt. Admittedly, I had kept Lying-Ass Larry a secret from most of my best friends for a long time, but that relationship had been a complete rollercoaster. Even when it was good, it was nothing like what Hannah and Devin appeared to have, so I truly couldn't imagine finding the love of my life and not feeling even remotely excited to tell my loved ones. The other side of me started to feel anger at the fact that Hannah didn't feel like she could even try to talk to us about how she was feeling. It made me wonder if she thought that we were so unreasonable or close-minded that we wouldn't be able to understand how she was feeling or admit that we were wrong for making her feel this way. After being best friends with Hannah for so long, I would have thought she'd known me better than to think that.

The longer I thought about it, the more I became anxious to talk to her about everything that was on my mind. Taking a deep breath, I had to remind myself once again that this was going to be a conversation for another day.

"It's okay, Ava, I can see you're upset, but just find some time to talk to Hannah about it, okay?" Leeta stated as she gave me a quick hug.

"Alright, what should we do about Sid's car?" Nina asked as she directed her attention to the empty parking lot.

"How about I take her car and follow you to her place, and then we come back together to come get Sid in my car. That way Nina can go home first," I suggested quickly.

"Are you guys sure?" Nina asked.

"Sounds great to me. Let's do it!" Leeta exclaimed as I nodded. Nina gave us both a thankful smile.

"Alright, but call me if you need me for anything okay? I'll turn right around," Nina replied firmly.

"Go, go and have your happily ever after with your wonderful husband," I cried out as we pushed Nina toward her car. We waved to her as she headed to her car alone before Leeta and I went to her and Sidney's cars. I turned on Sidney's Toyota and prayed she didn't wake up while we were gone and try to leave to find us.

The road was fairly empty with few cars on the road during the short drive from Big Ben's to Sidney's house. It was surprisingly nice to have a moment of peace and quiet to myself after spending literally all day dealing with problem after problem. We got back to Sidney's house without any hiccups, except the fact that I could see their bedroom light still on upstairs. I tried not to think about what that meant and parked her car before jumping into Leeta's without looking back. As we drove away, I gave Alex the middle finger out of the passenger window, which made Leeta cackle as we drove back to our best friend passed out in the parking lot.

The drive back with Leeta was relaxing after her laughter died down. She turned up the radio as we drove with the windows down under the night sky. For a few minutes, I was able to forget everything that happened today. It was like a short-lived escape until we pulled back into the parking lot. Leeta parked next to my car where Sidney's drooling face was smooshed against the window.

"Text me when you two get home?" Leeta said as she placed her hand on mine as I turned to leave.

"Yes, let me know when you get home too," I smiled back before stepping out.

I closed the door behind me before I walked around the front of Leeta's car to get to mine. It was cool inside my car and filled with the sound of Sidney's heavy snoring before I turned on the ignition to start it. Leeta waved one last time before driving off and leaving me behind as the last car in the parking lot.

"It's just you and me now, Sid."

I backed out of my parking spot and entered the main road to go back home. Rolling down my window, I let the chilly night breeze wash over me as I drove. Although I didn't normally drive with the windows down, it somehow felt relaxing tonight. We were all safe, and most of us were happy, and that was all I could ask for.

When we got back to my place, I had to use all of my yoga muscles to pull Sidney out of my car, who was now fully dead weight. I hoisted her arm around my shoulders and dragged her inside with all of the strength I could muster. It was a struggle balancing her with one arm as I tried to unlock my front door, but I somehow managed to get inside without dropping her. As my legs started to give, I threw her onto my couch, as it was the closest soft piece of furniture she could comfortably lay on. I took a moment to catch my breath before I went back to close my front door.

Pulling out my phone, I checked our group chat and saw that everyone had already made it home, so I updated the girls that Sidney and I had made it back safely too. Then I opened my private message thread with Hannah with my fingers hovered over the keyboard. I wasn't quite sure how I wanted to say what I wanted to say yet, but the first step I needed to make was to initiate.

Let me know when you're free to talk sometime.

When I checked on Sidney, she was starting to wake up and regain consciousness as she sleepily looked around my home, wondering where she was.

"How did I get here?" she questioned with her eyes half shut.

"Let's get you to bed," I replied, ignoring her question.

I took another deep breath before bending down to pick her up for what I hoped was the last time tonight. We made our way through the hallway and down to the guest bedroom across the hall from my bedroom. I kicked the door open and plopped her down onto the bed. Her hair was messily over her face as her loose limbs laid limp beside her on the bed. I picked up her legs and tucked her in like a child.

"Ava," Sidney whispered.

"Yes, Sid?"

"Why did he have to be in love with someone else?" she mumbled with the most sadness I'd heard from her all evening. Although her eyes were shut from drowsiness, tears began streaming down her face as she curled up in bed, holding onto the blanket under chin. She started to cry harder and harder as drool dribbled down her chin. I wiped her cheeks with a tissue from the nightstand and turned off the light, unsure of what to tell her.

Then, on my way out of her room, my phone rang from my pocket. When I checked who was calling me, low and behold it was Larry's daughter. Speak of the devil, or, well, the devil's daughter. I almost wanted to ignore the call, but the good in me knew better than to reject her call just because I was still mad at her father. In an attempt to be the better person, I answered the phone.

"Hey, Rebecca," I said quietly.

"Ava! Guess what? I finally found some really exciting internship opportunities that I want to apply for. Do you think you can help me update my resume?" she exclaimed with so much joy that I didn't have it in me to decline.

"Um, sure. What did you need help with?" The thing with Rebecca was that I was used to helping her when it came to college and her academics. To the shock of no one, Larry was completely useless when it came to assisting and guiding his daughter into adulthood, so somehow that meant it fell on my shoulders as a woman who dated him for a few months. I leaned against the door frame of my guest bedroom as Sidney's snoring resumed. We spent the next half hour going over the dos and don'ts, when Sidney woke up on her own.

"Is that Larry's daughter?" Sidney hissed as she slowly started opening her eyes.

"Shhh," I hushed as soon as I put the call on mute. "Yes, it is."

"Know what? We gotta talk about you still helping anyone in his family. I get it... no, I don't, not really. Fuck him and his entire bloodline. That's some bullshit!" Sidney shouted as she thrashed underneath the covers before sitting up.

"You're drunk, go back to bed. We'll discuss this in the morning," I scolded her as I tried to pay attention to Rebecca who was rambling on about some internship.

"We sure the hell will," Sidney snapped back as she fell back on her pillow. I shook my head and rubbed my temples as Rebecca tried to get my attention.

"Hello? Ava? Did you hear that?"

"Uh, no I didn't catch that. Can you repeat it?" I replied as I shut Sidney's door and entered my bedroom.

After another long hour on the phone with Larry's daughter, she finally had no more questions and was fully satisfied with her new resume. I got ready for bed as we spoke on the phone, taking off my makeup and changing into comfy pajamas to sleep in. The moment I was off the phone, I was finally free for the first time all day. I threw my exhausted body onto my bed and shut my eyes ready to get some well-deserved rest.

The last twenty-four hours had been one of the biggest rollercoasters I'd ever been on—and that even includes what happened with Lying-Ass Larry! From mental breakdowns with cleavers to hidden babies to the lack of babies to new fiancés who came out of nowhere, today was going to be a day I'd remember for the rest of my life. Whether it was for more good than bad reasons, I couldn't tell you.

All I could say was, "Siri, play Rain playlist on Tidal."

SCAN TO HEAR PLAYLIST

My Sisters

When morning came bright and early, I woke up feeling relieved that I'd survived the chaos that ensued the day before. A low groaning came from the guest bedroom from across the hall, telling me that Sidney was awake too. Judging by her painful moaning, I could only imagine what kind of awful hangover she was feeling. I got up out of bed and started to freshen up and get ready for the day before checking on my best friend. With a deep breath, I knocked on her door softly, to which she responded with a grunt. I pushed the door open slightly before I was assaulted with the stench of old margaritas emanating from Sidney's body.

"Oh my God, you smell awful," I cried out as I pinched my nose and waved fresh air in front of myself.

"I feel awful. Ava, I really think this is the end. My liver is finally giving up on me," Sidney replied dramatically as she pulled the covers over her head even higher.

"I wouldn't be surprised, with the night you had. You drank more than all of us and way later too," I chuckled as I leaned against the doorframe, watching Sidney suffer the worst hangover I'd ever witnessed in the last twenty years of our friendship.

"I had to catch up somehow," she pouted as she peeked her head out momentarily.

"Do you think you can make it to the kitchen?" I asked as I let out a huge yawn. I definitely needed coffee in my system asap.

"Absolutely not," she advised firmly from underneath the blanket.

"Alright, let me get you some coffee to revive," I chuckled.

"God, yes please."

I opened her bedroom door wider to ventilate the room as I went to the kitchen to make some coffee for the both of us and grab some ibuprofen for Sidney's pounding head. Leaning against the kitchen counter as the coffee brewed, I still couldn't stop thinking about everything that happened with Hannah. From her feeling like she couldn't talk to us to her surprise engagement, it was like I was in a boxing match with Mike Tyson, and he kept giving me the good ol' one-two punch over and over. With how unresolved things felt between Hannah and me, it made it a bit difficult to be as happy for her as I wanted to be. I pulled out my phone from my pocket and checked for any new messages, but there was nothing.

I guess she hadn't seen my text message yet...

My coffee machine finished so I put my phone back in my pocket and poured us each a large mug of coffee with sugar and cream before heading back to Sidney. When I returned, the room thankfully smelled a bit better than before with some air circulation. I sat down at Sidney's bedside and set her cup of coffee on the nightstand as she remained curled under the covers like a butterfly in a cocoon. Then I popped an ibuprofen pill out from the bottle and gently tapped Sidney on the shoulder.

"Come on, Sid, you gotta get up," I whispered as I tried to wake her up.

"Everything is better under here," she grumbled with a muffled voice.

"I have coffee," I sang.

"Good morning, my best friend in the whole wide world next to Nina, Leeta, and Hannah," Sidney cried out as she emerged from underneath the covers. I laughed as I handed her the pill and her coffee. She took a long sip, feeling the caffeine surge through her veins and begin to revive her body.

We sat together in the bed enjoying our coffees together peacefully. I was sure that there were more things she needed to get off of her chest about her divorce, but it didn't seem necessary to pressure her to talk about it when I knew she would come to me when she was ready. From the corner of my eye, I could see her stealing glances at me, which made me start to wonder if she was already feeling up to talking now. I turned to her and gave her a small smile.

"So…" Sidney finally started slowly. "Honestly, Ava, now that I've had a night to let everything start to sink in, I think I feel really good about this divorce. I'm not gonna pretend that it doesn't still hurt or that I'm completely over the shock of everything in the least bit, but if he's cheating on me with other women and full on in love with someone else, it's only better for myself that I move on to someone better," she admitted before taking another sip of coffee. Her voice was calm and steady, which made me feel confident that she was really feeling at ease about everything. She was right that when it came to a cheater, it was definitely easier to let go of the relationship, because why hold onto someone who didn't respect you?

"Agreed. He does not deserve someone like you, Sid," I nodded in agreement.

"But I'm just really worried about my kids," Sidney said as she dropped her voice with a heavy sigh.

"I totally forgot about them. They went to stay with your parents for the night, right?" I turned my whole body to her with worry.

"Yeah, Alex arranged it before he came home so that we could talk privately. I'm just really worried of it really messing them up. They're still pretty young, you know?" Sidney bit her lip as she looked down at her coffee.

"Let's just take things one step at a time first. First, let's focus on you and then we'll move on to what's best for the kids. At the end of the day, it's better to have two happy parents separately than two unhappy parents together," I told her in hopes that it would comfort her, but she was still clearly in distress with her forehead heavily creased as she tried to figure out an entire new life plan in the span of five minutes. As a mother, she was used to taking on the impossible, but figuring out a new life for her kids was rather ambitious.

"You're right… I just can't help but worry about what it'll do to them," she sighed in defeat as she tried to rack her brain of ideas, but of to no avail.

"How about—" I started, but before I could finish my thought, my phone rang in my pocket. I checked who was calling and it was Nina, so I answered the call right away.

"Hey, Nina," I greeted as I put her on speaker.

"Ava, I'm on the phone in a three-way call with Leeta and Hannah on the other line. Let me merge the calls together. Sidney is still with you, right?" Nina replied.

"Yeah, she is," I said as I glanced over at Sidney huddled over her coffee.

"I'm alive," she called out weakly. To say she was alive was quite literally all she was at this point. Sidney looked haggard with darkness under eyes and puffiness from all the drinking, but thankfully the coffee was starting to bring light back into her spirit.

"Alright, so I wanted to get everyone together to basically regroup after yesterday. Sidney, how are you feeling?" Nina asked on behalf of everyone on the call.

"Besides this hangover trying to kill me, a bit better," she chuckled with a low and hoarse voice.

"Makes sense. You thought you were a fish or something with how much you were drinking," Hannah commented, jabbing someone at their worst yet again.

"Okay, we don't need to focus on how much I drank last night," Sidney pressed firmly.

"Why don't we all meet up at Ava's place to talk?" Nina suggested, breaking up the tangents from the more important issue at hand: what Sidney was going to do following the divorce.

"Yeah, come over. Don't think Sid is any condition to go anywhere else at this point," I agreed and gave Sid the side eye.

"Hey!" she argued back before dropping her voice back to normal. "But true, please come."

"Alright, heading over," Nina confirmed.

"See you soon," Leeta said before hanging up.

While the girls made their way over to my place, I tried my best to get Sidney out of bed. She needed to get some food in her system and, if possible, a shower. I grabbed a towel for her and some clean clothes to borrow and laid it out on the comforter beside her as she drank coffee in bed with her eyes closed.

"Okay, Sid. You gotta shower before they get here. You stink of alcohol," I told her as I tried to pull her out of bed. However, this only made her recoil under the covers even more.

"Can I just stay here?" she asked, curled up like a little bunny in a burrow.

"No," I replied flatly like a military sergeant.

We both started cracking up as I took her coffee from the nightstand and placed it across the room from her. If she wanted any more, she needed to get out of bed to get it. Sidney groaned as she picked herself up out of bed and finally started to get on with her day. While she freshened up, I went to the kitchen to whip us up a quick breakfast with whatever I had lying around.

I dug through the cabinets and fridge and found I had near to nothing—as usual. At the very least, I thought I might've had some eggs and toast but because I forgot that I almost never cooked at home, all I had in the pantry were some protein bars, so I pulled those out and started snacking on one as I placed a delivery order for bagels and donuts.

Almost forty minutes later, everyone arrived at my place, along with the delivery person for our breakfast. The ladies piled into my living room and gathered around on the couch as I placed the food in the center and started brewing more coffee. Shortly after, Sidney came out of the bathroom with a towel around her neck, wearing my pajamas. Nina, Hannah, and Leeta gathered around Sidney for a group hug to comfort her, but Sidney's eyes were glued to the coffee machine in the kitchen for her second cup of joe.

Once all settled into our seats around my living room, I took a bite out of a bagel, letting the sweet morning carbs energize me.

"So, not to be a downer, but just to get down to business, what are you gonna do about your divorce? Do you have a plan for your kids, Sidney? When do you think you will tell them about the divorce?" Nina asked in a spitfire of questions that none of us were ready for. We sat in silence and let Nina do the talking. Sidney poured herself another cup of coffee and blew on it as she thought about Nina's questions.

After a long pause, she finally said, "I have no idea. They're still in elementary school, so I'm scared. What if it makes them withdraw or something? Divorce is always the hardest on kids, you know?" She shook her head as she continued to run through various scenarios about what she could do. I watched Sidney's expression grow dark as she thought about how much this would change her children's' lives. Divorce was never something anyone dealt with easily, especially as kids when they were too young to understand why mommy and daddy didn't love each other anymore. It was then that the thought of Sidney being a divorcee really sunk in for all of us, including Sidney. It was easy to think about leaving the man who cheated on you until you had to actually go through the logistics of it when he was also the father of your children.

"If it means anything to you, I think you'll be a great single mom. It's tough at first, but our kids are always worth the extra work," Hannah commented, breaking the silence. We all looked at her in surprise and pride. It was one of the first times she'd said something really good at the right time. Perhaps being engaged was changing

Hannah already, and thankfully for the better!

"Thanks, Hannah, I really appreciate that. You've been a great single mom, but I'm so happy for Sara that she's about to have a new daddy!" Sidney sang happily as she glanced at Hannah's enormous engagement ring.

"Yeah, Sid. You're a great mom, and whatever happens will work out. Plus, you have all of us if you ever need any help," Leeta added as she rubbed Sidney's leg warmly.

"Alright, enough about me. I'm still so hungover. Let's talk about someone else now. How's everything with you and Michael, Nina?" She exclaimed as she waved off the sentimental feelings and turned to Nina.

"Honestly… it went fantastic," Nina confessed with a shy smile. Her cheeks flushed red, so she covered her face with a pillow and giggled like a little schoolgirl.

"That's amazing!" We all cheered in excitement.

"So, when I got home, Michael was on the couch waiting for me, even though he's normally super tired after work and usually goes to sleep early, we talked on the couch for probably two hours about how much I've been struggling with having trouble conceiving and he was so sweet about everything. We're still gonna continue trying for one more year, but if it doesn't happen, then that's okay. We're both open to adoption, so in a few months we're gonna start researching the adoption process and see if we can get approved!" She exclaimed the great news behind the pillow, causing all of us to scream. Leeta jumped up from the couch and bounced around Nina, unable to contain herself from the news. Hannah and I grabbed each other's hands at the same time, screaming like children on Christmas day.

Sidney pulled Nina into the biggest hug, welcoming her into the motherhood club.

"OMG, NINA!" Leeta cried out as she danced around the room.

"So, hopefully, we'll get to be parents within the next two years. Fingers crossed!" Nina beamed the brightest I'd ever seen her in a very long time. We all had been able to tell there'd been a little trouble going on behind the scenes in her marriage, but it was such a relief to know that all it took was some communication to resolve everything, and now things between her and Michael were even better than they were before.

"That's so great! I'm so happy for you," Sidney cheered as she proposed a toast with her coffee. We all raised our mugs and turned to Nina. "To Nina becoming a mom!"

"Thanks, you guys, I can't believe it either, truthfully. I've always wanted to be a mom so bad, and it's finally gonna happen! Well, maybe, but hopefully!" Nina cried out as we clinked our cups together and took a much-needed dose of caffeine.

Although we were all excited for Nina and her new journey toward being a mom, I still couldn't help but feel the looming gray feeling on my thoughts about Hannah. So, it was hard to be fully present in the conversation despite all of the good news. From the corner of my eye, I could see that Sidney noticed my absentmindedness. She nudged me and raised an eyebrow as she continued to celebrate Nina's big news. Even though she'd been way too drunk last night to be aware of how I felt about Hannah hiding her man from us for so long, she could tell right away that something was clearly on my mind.

"Hey, so I think Ava might have something to say too," Sidney announced to the group. Everyone turned to me as I stared at her, shocked with wide eyes that she would put me on blast like that. Sidney simply smiled back and took a sip of her coffee innocently.

"What's up, Ava?" Hannah asked.

"Um, so I wanted to talk to you about Devin. Well, more specifically, how you said you felt about keeping your relationship a secret," I started off hesitantly. Talking about this in front of our other best friends didn't bother me or make me feel uncomfortable, but I'd been caught off guard by Sidney. I wanted to talk to Hannah asap, but I didn't expect today to be the day.

"Oh," she breathed.

"Firstly, I just wanted to say I'm sorry that we ever made you feel like you couldn't share something so big in your life. I know we've said a lot of stuff about Black men, but you deserve happiness regardless of what we think. What matters is how you feel and you being truly happy. Plus, in your situation, we were wrong anyway. Devin seems like such a good person and very clearly your perfect other half," I said as I grabbed her hand gently.

"I agree with Ava. Maybe we were too harsh because of the way things didn't work out with us," Leeta continued.

"We'll be more mindful of the way we say things, but I hope moving forward that if any of us ever feel this way again that we feel comfortable enough to speak up. We're best friends, and it's important that we feel comfortable enough to be honest and communicate our feelings," Nina summed up as Hannah and I hugged out our feelings.

"Thanks, guys. I know I should have spoken up sooner if it was bothering me for so long. I'll try to do better too," Hannah said as she smiled at everyone.

"But onto better news, I still am in shock about your proposal, Hannah," Sidney chimed in, loosening up the serious mood again.

"You're in shock? I'm in shock! I really had no clue he was going to pull out a ring!" Hannah exclaimed as she held out her hand and stomped her feet giddily.

"It's got to be at least three and a half carats," Leeta gasped in awe as she looked over the ring sparkling in the daylight. It was even more beautiful now that we could fully see all of the details with natural lighting instead of the bar's dim lighting.

"No, five carats," Hannah corrected.

"Hot damn, I knew it! I know diamonds!" Nina exclaimed as she applauded herself and jumped up and down with excitement. We all couldn't stop laughing at Nina parading about her own triumph amidst Hannah's proposal.

I also joined in on the laughter and celebration now that I finally felt at peace with my feelings about Hannah's situation. Of course, we still needed to have a one-on-one conversation just between us, but for the most part, I felt content with what we were able to talk about for now, since I was able to get the big things on my mind off of my chest.

"I'm not gonna lie, Devin is so fine. How did you get such a good-looking man, and where can I get one? Lord knows I need one now that I'm getting rid of mine," Sidney stated before casually taking a bite of a donut from the table.

For a moment, we all froze at Sidney's comment, unsure of whether or not it was a joke we were allowed to laugh at. Hannah forced an awkward chuckle while I turned to look at Sidney for any direction. She shrugged her shoulders at me and took another sip of her coffee before shimmying her shoulders as the caffeine continued to course her veins. I gave her another look, telepathically urging her to say something.

"Guys, it's a joke. You can laugh," Sidney finally replied nonchalantly.

"Oh my God, Sid. I know it's your divorce, but that was way too soon, even for me," Nina confessed as she held onto her chest. Although we knew Sidney extremely well, we'd never dealt with heartbroken Sidney, so we all wanted to tread lightly around her divorce.

"I gotta have some fun somehow, right?" She smiled, reassuring us that she was going to be okay.

"That's true. Divorce is messy, but you can't be sad about it forever. Amen to that," Hannah cheered her coffee with Sidney. The two women took a sip of their coffee before munching on the donuts in unison. It was so nice watching my best friends, although going through two polar opposite situations, still had something to celebrate together. Times like these reminded me exactly why the five of us were going to be friends until our graves.

"I know, and I won't be sad forever. Maybe just a little for now, but I'm allowed to be sad and make bad jokes for now. Wounds are fresh," Sidney clarified to the room as she waved around her donut with crumbs around her mouth. "But that wasn't the news I was talking about," Sidney continued as she shook her head.

"What do you mean?" Leeta questioned with a puzzled expression.

"Ava has an update with Lying-Ass Larry! Or, well, his daughter

Rebecca," she replied as she cocked her head in my direction. Sidney sat back on the couch with her donut like a movie watcher with popcorn about to enjoy a show.

"WHAT!" Everyone else in the room cried out as they whipped their heads in my direction all at once.

"He's still in the picture?" Hannah asked, but in a tone that really said "girl, are you out of your damn mind?"

"Right? Even my drunk ass knew better than for her to pick up his daughter's call last night," Sidney said, which only added more gasoline to the fire.

I slowly turned my head to Sidney in complete shock. Here I thought she was still recovering, and I needed to be a little nicer to her because of her divorce, yet she's the one putting me on blast for something I had completely forgotten about.

"Were you gonna wait forever to tell us like you did about Larry?" Nina scolded as she folded her arms and gave me a stern look.

"It wasn't a big deal. It's just in my DNA to help young adults, especially young Black talent, you guys know that," I replied, feeling cornered all at once. At the time, it didn't seem like such a big deal because I loved helping Rebecca, even if it wasn't always convenient to do so or because of her good for nothing father.

"But you don't find it weird to be helping your ex's, or whatever he was, kid so much?" Hannah questioned, again her tone proving she was really saying something completely different. What she meant to say was, "It's really weird to be helping your ex's kid so much, Ava."

"He was not my ex. He was nothing to me as I didn't even know who he was. And actually, no I don't. The more I think about it, the more I feel like maybe I keep helping her because it's my true calling," I confessed for the first time since realizing these feelings of mine. It wasn't like I hated my job being a businesswoman, but there was something about helping young Black talent that made me feel satisfied with my work.

"Your true calling?" Leeta asked.

"I really think that maybe I should be helping young people figure out their full potential. I know Rebecca isn't the most ideal person to be helping, but she's not her dad, and I don't think it's fair to hold her back just because of something personal that happened between me and that idiot father of her's," I explained, to which I received multiple nods from everyone in response except for Hannah.

"Ever think there's a chance between you and Larry?" Hannah wondered. Everyone scooted forward closer to me, clearly thinking the same thing as her.

"I can't stand or stomach to hear that niccas' name, let alone see him, but Rebecca is not Larry," I clarified as I closed my eyes and covered my ears. The last thing I wanted was to keep thinking about him like this, which was one of the main reasons why I kept the situation with him a secret for so long.

"You're better than me. There ain't enough high road in this world for me to help her. God is still working on me," Leeta exclaimed as she crossed her legs and exhaled deeply

Nina, Hannah, and I were all extremely taken back by Leeta's comment. She was our human care-bear, so none of us ever expected her to say something like that. But like all of the other struggles in our lives, there was nothing else we could do but laugh it off. At the end of the day, finding humor amidst our troubles was all any of us could do to continue pushing forward. If we didn't find something to joke about or poke fun at, then we'd just be at home miserable every day. It took us a long time to understand that, perhaps maybe even until our forties, but it was true when people said there wasn't enough time in life to take it so seriously all of the time.

"This is why I'm single. I can't, I'd kill somebody. I can't imagine being Larry's wife. I actually feel sorry for her," I said as I shook my head.

"Shiiiittt, in today's world, she may know and don't care. She might just be happy to have a piece of a man," Sidney countered.

"Yeah, you got a point there," we recited in unison as we all shook our heads in disappointment.

"Real talk, Ava, you might have met your Boaz a long time ago if you weren't screwing your other 'best friend' for years," Hannah replied, unprovoked by anyone. Apparently, she was back to her old bad timing self again. I slapped my hand to my forehead for mistakenly thinking otherwise before.

The room erupted with even more laughter, to the point that Sidney spat out her coffee across the room. It dribbled down her chin like she was a child while a fresh mist of coffee coated the table.

"I forgot about that scandal," Sidney gasped.

"I didn't," Nina, Leeta, and Hannah all said together at once. I glared at Hannah with scolding eyes.

"It's always you, Hannah, always you," I remarked as I narrowed my eyes, shook my head, and pointed a stern finger at her.

"I just keep it real," she replied with a smirk and flicked her blonde hair over her shoulder.

"Well, that's over. It's been over. It was just something we both needed at that time. He's one of my best friends and I will always love him for being just that, no matter what." I exhaled deeply as I took another bite of my bagel and washed it down with some coffee.

"For damn near ten years' worth of time," Hannah clarified like a common-law marriage. *"You say we're just friends, but I swear when nobody's around ... or whatever Khalid said,"* Hannah sang.

"Shut up, Hannah," I shouted playfully and threatened her with my bagel. "Anyways, let's talk about something else," I stated in hopes of changing the conversation to something far, far away from me and my lack of love life. However, everyone else sat back on the couch with their lips pressed tight as they darted their eyes back and forth between Hannah and me. No one wanted to say anything, as they enjoyed the drama unfolding before their eyes. It was like watching live reality television for the three of them.

"You heard from Big Boy Porn Star Rick?" Leeta asked me innocently, breaking the long pause.

I just shook my head and threw my hands in the air feeling defeated.

Lovers, Friends & Securing Your Own Mask

I rolled my eyes at Leeta for bringing up Rick. He was truly one of a kind, but not in the sense everyone was thinking—Rick was a true friend kind of love. There was something about him and the way he was able to listen and participate in the conversation that made me feel comfortable enough to really talk about anything and everything under the sun, just like I did with my best friends. Before Rick, I always had a bit of trouble fully believing that a man and a woman could be just friends, but having Rick as a friend proved me wrong. I think that was the biggest lesson when I think back to my time with him. Ultimately, not all relationships are meant to be romantic, no matter how in tune you are together or how much you click. And there's nothing wrong or unhealthy about that.

"You can't tell me that there wasn't a small part of you that wanted more with Rick," Hannah tried to pry as she narrowed her eyes at me suspiciously. Rick was definitely one of the better-looking people I've dated, so it was hard for anyone to believe I wasn't attracted to him that way. Well, I mean, he was fine as hell to look at with a package superseding expectation, but the chemistry just wasn't where it needed to be.

"Actually, I can. I mean, we did have sex once, but that was it. And don't get me wrong, it was great, but it just didn't have that spark I needed to prove to myself that we were meant for each other in that kind of way. He was just someone I needed at that time," I explained, but all I received in return were four equally confused faces looking back at me. It was like I was trying to talk to them in a foreign language with how lost they all looked. None of them had any purely platonic friends of the opposite sex like I did, except for a few queer friends who were not interested in them for obvious reasons.

"I respect that, but I just don't think I'll ever fully get it," Nina admitted with a chuckle. The rest of the girls nodded their heads in agreement, so I decided to break it down even more for them to better understand.

"It's kind of like if I were to sleep with one of you guys," I said plainly.

"What?" They all cried out with wide eyes.

"Just hear me out. I'm able to fully be myself and talk to you guys about anything. If there were non-romantic soulmates, it would be you guys, but even though we get each other the way other people never will, it doesn't mean I'm in love with you guys that way or want to sleep with any of you," I clarified more specifically.

"Oh, I guess that makes sense," Hannah agreed.

"Rick and I genuinely cared for each other, and we've told each other that, but that's really all there is to it," I stated. My best friends all nodded their heads as my explanation started to sink into their brains. If you told me the same thing just a few years ago, I would have responded the same way Nina did. Finding a platonic love in the opposite sex, especially when you'd already had a physical relationship with them, sounded near impossible. However, after living it myself, I realized how possible it really could be.

Love came in all forms, and there wasn't one type of love that was more important than any other, because romantic love wasn't the only kind of love we need in life.

"I guess there's more to love than just romance," Sidney sighed. Romantic love was pretty much all she knew, as someone who married right out of college, but that was the beauty in having friends and being able to talk about these kinds of deep topics together. What we didn't learn in our own lives, we were able to learn from each other.

"I think so. After my one night with Rick, I thought a lot about this and I wish I knew this when I was in my twenties, but romantic love isn't everything. It's great and is an irreplaceable form of love in our lives, but it's not the only important form of love in our lives," I replied. There were so many things I wished my younger self knew, but there was no turning back the clock now. The only important thing was that I knew what I needed to know now and could apply to my life moving forward.

"That's true. You have platonic love like Ava and Rick," Hannah added.

"You have familial love like Sidney and her kids," Leeta continued.

"And you have self-love," Nina smiled.

"But we also can't forget about how important it is to be open and honest with ourselves about loving who we love. We all have our own preconceived notions about what we think we want or what we think is good for each other, but sometimes you just never know who's gonna walk in through the door and change your mind about everything," I said, feeling quite in the philosophical mood after spending the morning talking about love.

"Amen to that," Hannah agreed as she raised her cup.

"If I could also get an amen to me one day getting my own Devin, that would be great, Dear Father," Sidney chimed in as she pressed her hands together in prayer and looked up at the sky.

"Sidney!" Nina gasped and softly smacked her shoulder for her ridiculousness.

"What? I'm just asking," Sidney retorted.

"It's also important not to let societal pressure get to you either," Leeta commented as she completely ignored both Nina and Sidney, who often had a cat and mouse type of relationship, so to see their back and forth like this was nothing new to any of us after almost twenty years, it only made us laugh watching them.

"That's right, Leeta. There is no timeline everyone has to follow about when they find a life partner, or if they even have to have a partner at all. It's up to us and what we want and need that matters, not what other people think." I nodded. This piece of advice was most prevalent to Leeta and I as the only ones without any prospect of marriage in the near future. It was good to remember that whether or not we got married or found our perfect person, it was entirely up to us and it didn't matter at what age it happened.

"Exactly! Plus, just because you 'do everything right' according to society doesn't mean you'll end up happy anyway," Sidney remarked, clearly hinting at the failure of her own marriage, especially after seventeen years of seemingly being happily married.

"Shit happens. No one's life is perfect," Hannah summarized bluntly as she shrugged with a smile.

"You just gotta learn to trust your intuition," Nina said. All of our brains were firing off all of the things we'd learned in our lifetime like it was a support group for AA. However, none of us minded it. In fact, it made me even happier than when we got together and just talked about work and our daily lives. It was good to have a deep heart to heart talk about our ups and downs, our triumphs and shortcomings in order to grow and help each other grow every so often. I sat back and beamed at my best friends as we basked in our collective knowledge and wisdom.

"Yeah, God only knows where you'd be with Larry's lying ass if you didn't trust your gut," Sidney continued as she directed her attention to me.

"Don't remind me…" I groaned as I shut my eyes momentarily. "But I'm glad things didn't work out with him." I wiped my forehead of imaginary sweat as I thought about how much I dodged a bullet.

"You'll find someone out there for you. Hannah didn't settle and look at what a fine man she found," Leeta cheered as she grinned at Hannah and me. Our little care-bear never failed to say the right thing to cheer me up.

"Lord, are you listening?" Sidney cried out as she tilted up to the ceiling a second time. She waved her hand in hopes God was watching as she put in her request for her own personal Devin.

"I was talking about for Ava, but I guess you too," Leeta said as she shook her head at Sidney's silliness, but it all just made us giggle.

"As grateful as I am to have found Devin now, I think a small part of me in the back of my mind always knew that I was settling with my exes. As if I didn't deserve better, which was why I stayed with them for so long. Neither of them were particularly great people, but it was easy and I was scared of potentially realizing I didn't deserve more. But now that I know that wasn't true, I'm so much happier with Devin," Hannah revealed with a bashful smile. Just thinking about Devin was enough to make her entire demeanor change, and for the better too. Her happiness was so vibrant it was practically glowing off of her because she finally found self-love for herself and it allowed her to find her first healthy romantic relationship.

"I think the issue might have been the difference between compromise and settling. Let's face it, every relationship has to have compromise. If there's no compromise, you're just gonna fight all of the time. But there is a line where there's too much compromise and it just becomes settling. Both parties have to win and lose some, it can't just be one sided all of the time," Nina started to explain. "Hell, I just learned that myself with Michael last night. I was taking on so much by myself that I wasn't prioritizing how I was feeling, all because I didn't want to burden him. But that's not healthy in a relationship," she continued.

I nodded in agreement as I realized that I had done the exact same thing myself. So many times, I gave too much without even realizing that my partner was nowhere near giving enough back. All it took was Nina putting those feelings into words for me to really understand that feeling.

"You're right. I think that's what happened with my exes. I was always finding myself having to apologize or give in to their wants and needs, even when it went against what I wanted and needed. Because I 'loved' them, I thought it was okay to put my feelings aside for the sake of no longer fighting," I confessed as I had my epiphany.

"I'm so glad you know that now, because that's so important to grasp, especially going into a marriage," Nina concluded with a bright smile. Although I wasn't getting married anytime soon, she was right that this was definitely something I needed to learn before I did.

"It's important to know even if you don't get married though, because not everyone wants to get married," Leeta joined in, which surprised us.

"Woah, Leeta, is there something you want to tell us?" Hannah wondered.

"Well, now that I'm in my forties, I've learned that I just don't care about marriage as much as I did when I was in my twenties or my thirties. Of course, I'd love to have someone to grow old with, but I'm starting to realize I don't need someone to tell me that my love with someone is more real just because a piece of paper says so," Leeta replied confidently.

"I guess that's true. Love is love, no matter what," I agreed and rubbed her arm in support.

"I thought I needed marriage to feel that," Leeta continued. "That spark of love like a romance novel or something, but I don't think I do. As long as I have a partner for life who will love and cherish me for the rest of our lives together, then that's all I care about."

"Good for you, Leeta! You're right, it really doesn't matter what a piece of paper says if you know what you have is right for you," Sidney cheered in another silent "fuck you" to Alex.

"Exactly! Love needs to be enjoyed, and no one should be able to tell me how to do that," Leeta said proudly as she sat up tall in her seat.

"Wow, I never really thought about it that way. 'Love needs to be enjoyed.' I love that," Hannah replied in awe as she made a mental note of that quote.

"I read it in a book about a woman navigating her love life as an adult, and it really stuck with me. I feel like a lot of times, we take love for granted in a sense. Like it's a collectable we need to have just for sake of having instead of something to cherish," Leeta explained. It was incredible to see how much growth Leeta had made over the last few years as she recited the lessons she'd learned from that book like a college professor. "And most importantly, we gotta remember to love ourselves first. It's like how airplane safety works. You have to secure your own mask before trying to secure the mask of others."

"I'll admit that it took a long time for me to learn to love myself," Nina revealed with a heavy sigh.

"Really? I would have never guessed, because you've always seemed so sure of yourself!" Hannah gasped as she took a double take at Nina.

"Well, being sure of myself and loving myself are still pretty different. I know that I can be a lot sometimes, even too much for people at times, but it's hard to let my guard down and let others take control. That's kinda why I always need things to be perfect, even though I know I'm far from it myself," Nina said as she dropped her gaze and fiddled with her fingers on her lap. It was scary for her to be this vulnerable, and rightfully so. Talking about our deepest feelings was always terrifying because you never knew how people were going to perceive it, but I was so happy that being in a room full of her best friends made her feel safe enough to speak up about it. "I think it wasn't until my thirties that I started realizing that I'm perfectly fine the way I am. Everyone has good and bad to them, even things that they're not proud to admit it, but it doesn't make us any less of who we are or why we should love ourselves."

"Amen to that, Nina!" We all cheered.

"It's so crazy how hard it is to learn self-love when it's so important! I struggled with self-love too, and I wish my forty-something year old self could tell my twenty-something year old self that no one is ever going to love me the way that I love me. We're with ourselves a hundred percent of the time, every year, all year, since birth and till the day we die. If we're not okay with who we are, then how can we expect anyone else to be? The way we love ourself is the way we allow someone else to love us, and I wish so damn much that I knew that through all of those crappy relationships I endured in my youth. All I needed to do was learn how to love myself and everything else would fall in place," Leeta exclaimed, intensely engrossed in the topic. She was never one to raise her voice, but to see her so passionate about something that really mattered was almost inspiring to watch.

"Self-love is one of the most important types of love, but you also gotta remember there are sometimes just asshole men out there, like Larry or Alex. There are definitely good men out there like Michael and Devin, but no matter what man comes our way, our own self-worth comes first. Whether that means looking for love or not, it's about what we want for ourselves, on our own terms, not what anyone else says we have to do. We are grown ass women, why do we need to be listening to other people's nonsense anyway? If you're single, it's okay to be single. If you're married, it's okay to be married. If you're divorced, it's okay to be divorced. Whatever is meant for you is meant for you, and only you can determine that," I added in continuation to Leeta's last point, and it felt so good to get that off of my chest as well as share it with my girlfriends.

It'd been such a long time since the five of us had gotten together to sit down and talk about our thoughts and feelings about life and love like this. Although all of the troubles and hardships that happened over the last few weeks weren't ideal, it secretly made me happy how much we were able to see each other again regardless of the circumstances. As we'd gotten older, we increasingly lost time for each other because of how busy our lives became and how different the directions our lives took, but going through breaks-ups, divorces, infertility, and engagements together showed me that nothing had really changed between us and making time for each other wasn't as hard as we thought it was. And, most importantly, we were able to overcome anything as long as we were together.

I sat back in my seat and admired my best friends happily chatting together as I sipped on my coffee. We all ended up taking off work that day to hang out at my place like how we used to in our twenties. There was so much we had learned together and still so much left to learn, but what mattered most was that we had each other by our sides for every step of the way. Although I had worked hard and pushed myself to get to where I was in my life, there was no doubt that I also wouldn't be where I was without my best friends supporting me the whole way there.

We ended up ordering lunch and dinner so that we could continue talking about our thoughts and feelings about life without any interruption. It was kind of like the best Ted Talk of our lives with how much knowledge we'd each individually accumulated and were able to share with each other so we could learn from one another.

Later in the evening, Sidney received a call in the middle of dinner from her parents saying they were on their way to drop off her kids, so she decided it was finally time to go back home and face Alex again. We asked her if she was sure, but she insisted she was fine, especially since she wasn't the one who did anything wrong. Alex was going to have to be the one to pack up his things and move out in the meantime, not her. So, before she left, we gave her one last group hug for support. Nina volunteered to drop her off at home since Leeta and I drove last night, so they got in Nina's car together while Leeta and Hannah left in their own cars. I waved to all of them from my door.

After everyone was gone, I closed the door and went back to the living room to clean up the leftovers on the coffee table. While I was packing up the food, I grabbed my phone, "Siri, play Just Fine by Mary J. Blige on Tidal."

SCAN TO HEAR SONG

Thanks to technology and Bluetooth, the music was bangin' at the perfect level, and as usual, Mary J. Blige had me boppin' around – as I put the remaining leftovers in the fridge. One can always count on the amazing Mary to get you in whatever mood you needed to be in. Music is life, and her music is a whole mood!

Afterwards, I pulled out a glass and a bottle of Pinot Grigio by Opulence Wine. Just as I took a seat on one of the kitchen barstools, there was a knock at the door. I paused, wondering if someone had left something behind, so I put the glass of wine down and briskly walked back to the door.

"Ava Amore?" A man in a blue uniform questioned as he looked down at the order sheet in his hand while he carried a bouquet of fresh flowers in the other.

"That's me," I replied as I raised my hand instinctually like I was back in school.

"Please sign here," he requested as he handed me the order form. I looked it over but didn't see anyone's name except for the florist company.

"Thanks," I said as the man handed me the bouquet of flowers wrapped in clear plastic and light purple tissue paper. It was so large, it barely fit in my arms as I counted. There were three dozen lavender roses, which were my favorite flower. Their sweet, floral aroma filled my nose as I dove my face in the bouquet. In the center, was a small card poking out in between the petals. As I pulled my face back, I reached for the card and returned to the kitchen to sit down and read it aloud.

"I miss you. I still love you, always" it said.

The card was unsigned, but there was no doubt in my mind who they were from. Although it had been a while since I thought about him in that way, it didn't mean I still didn't love and miss him from time to time. Instantly, my cheeks flushed deep red as I sat back in my seat and rested my head on my shoulders thinking about him.

After everything my friends and I had talked about, my perception about love and life had definitely shifted in a way I didn't expect it to. I was already confident in myself and my self-worth, but hearing everyone's stories and struggles only confirmed what I already knew—there's no such thing as a perfect life, perfect relationship, or perfect "path." Life is what you make it. Don't let society sway your views or dictate your journey, they're just as f—ked up as you are; perfectly imperfect!

Funnily enough, hearing from him again was exactly what I needed to push me in the right direction to do what was right for me. I am going to live my life on my terms because I am single, not sorry, and one hundred percent proud of it.

"Siri, play Glamorous Life by Sheila E on Tidal."

SCAN TO HEAR SONG

Additional Recipes

Whatever your mood, drink with us, laugh with us, and enjoy responsibly ☺ ...

TOXIC
Henny-Rita

Materials needed: shaking tin w/top, ice, lime cut, glass
Alcohol needed: Hennessy, Grand Marnier, sour mix (nonalcoholic)

First grab your mixing tin, add ice, and then add:
5 count (4.5 oz) Hennessy
3 count (1.5oz) Grand Marnier
1 count (.5oz) sour mix
Shake, pour in glass, garnish with lime!

EMOTIONAL ROLLERCOASTER
Watermelon Refresher

Materials needed: ice, mixing tin, cucumbers sliced, highball glass
Nonalcoholic: watermelon purée, agave sour
Alcohol: Effen (cucumber flavor), watermelon pucker

Grab mixing tin combine ice, 4 count (2oz) Effen, a dash of agave sour (.5oz), 2 count (1oz) watermelon pucker, 2 count (1oz) watermelon purée.
Shake, pour in highball glass, garnish with cucumber!

DELUSIONAL
Chocolate Irish Coffee (hot or cold)

Materials needed: your favorite coffee brand, coffee mug, spoon
Alcohol: Baileys, Patron coffee liqueur

Pour your favorite coffee in a mug a little over halfway, grab 4 count (2oz) of Baileys, 2 count (1oz) of Patron coffee liqueur
Stir. Be careful, it tastes like hot chocolate, but it has a helluva kick!

F*CK IT
Cinnamon Toast

Materials needed: mixing tin, shot glass, ice
Alcohol: Baileys, Fireball

Grab mixing tin, ice, pour in 3 count (1.5oz) Fireball, a dash of Baileys (.5oz), shake. Strain in shot glass.
Drink responsibly! Fireball has a 40% alcohol content.

HONORABLE MENTION
Strawberry Mule

Materials needed: cooper mug, ice, lime, mixing tin
Alcohol needed: Tito's
Nonalcoholic: Ginger beer, strawberry purée

Grab your mixing tin, add ice, Tito's 5 count (2.5oz), 2 count (1oz) strawberry purée, shake and pour into the cooper mug, then fill the remaining mug with Ginger Beer, garnish with lime!

All drink recipes provided by licensed mixologist, Rotasha Allen.

Author's Playlist

SCAN TO HEAR PLAYLIST

About the Author

Much-like the main character, Ava Amore, Jennifer is a single, heterosexual woman in her forties. Although she's having a great time dating, there's still no potential life-partner in sight.

In her early twenties, Jennifer began her career in Corporate America, working her way up the ladder in Human Resources. Currently, as a senior leader in advertising, Jennifer spends her days leading diversity, equity, inclusion, and accessibility initiatives. And much like Ava, she too is an "employed entrepreneur" and has run a thriving communications consulting company for over ten years.

A single parent to one, over the years Jennifer devoted most of her time and energy to her son, work, school, and various passion projects. But something rattled her when she turned forty—the same year her son graduated high school and was declared "legally grown." She began to feel a little empty inside, wondering if her decision to fully embrace "singlehood" over the past fifteen years had been the right choice.

But what, exactly, is considered right? Who on earth qualifies to validate what's right or wrong when it comes to being single, in a partnership, married, separated, or divorced? No one.

Society will have you thinking, if you're bigger than a size four, you're fat. If you don't have at least 100,000 followers on social media, you're irrelevant. And if you aren't married with children by the age of thirty-five, it sucks to be you. Something must be wrong with you. You might-as-well hang it up, it's too late!

"I want women to stop putting so much pressure on themselves trying to live up to family, friends, and/or societal expectations. Who are they? No one, just another human like you and I," says Jennifer.

Not too long ago, a dear friend told Jennifer that she needed to relax her standards a bit. Quit being so difficult because she's now past her prime and halfway over the hill. It was then that Jennifer had had enough. That was all the motivation she needed to finish this book.

This dramatic, interpersonal, somewhat-fiction work doesn't stop at storytelling. It provides you with access to customized playlists and adult-beverage recipes created for the mood. It's an experience!

Ava Amore and friends tell the story of love, lust, lies, loss, and living. Sing with us. Rock with us. Drink with us—and enjoy!

www.ingramcontent.com/pod-product-compliance
Lightning Source LLC
Chambersburg PA
CBHW020333260626
47156CB00004B/1506